The

Master

Chef

Mark Anthony

Forward

This book contains the use of flashbacks between past and present events. The flashbacks generally occur at the beginning of a chapter, or after an awakening from a dream in the midst of a chapter. To make the flashbacks easily identifiable, each one is preceded by the symbols ...<<... ...>>... to indicate either a *flashback* or a *flash forward*.

We also want to present the disclaimer that while the biblical truths and principles presented in this book are certain, the presentation of the future events are merely speculative. We recommend that the reader study the word of God for a greater understanding of end-time events and chronology. Time truly is short and it is critical for each of us to learn for ourselves what the Bible says. As we approach the close of time, deception will not be perceived without a genuine knowledge of scripture. Read, study, and pray as never before. It will change your life... for eternity.

Chapters

Flashbacks

The sound of crashing plates echoed loudly from the dish room with its stainless counters and Marlite walls, startling the patrons of the greasy spoon full of truckers enjoying their chicken fried steaks, fried eggs and thick stacks of syrup laden pancakes. Jenny quickly excused herself from a four-top about to order to see what all the commotion was about. She rushed by the kitchen, seeing no one attending to the griddle and knew something was wrong.

The screams for help were muffled by Jenny's own panic as she raced into the dish room and saw her husband on the cold tile floor, surrounded by broken china. Steve was holding Phil's shaking body as Lisa stood by.

"I'll call 911!" Edith gasped, rushing by Jenny.

"Phil!" Jenny shouted as she rushed to his side.

Seeing a laceration or burn would have been a relief, but the pale fist clutched tightly to Phil's chest indicated something far more severe. Phil looked up at his wife of twenty years with a compassion in his eyes that revealed more concern for her than for himself. Another wave of clutching and jolting signaled that the worst was not over. Phil was sweating profusely and turning as pale as the wintery snow that blanketed this little Midwest town in the February cold.

"I'll get some towels!" Lisa offered.

"The paramedics are on their way," Edith said. "Help is coming."

With every shallow breath Phil took, the feeling of helplessness grew. Lisa came back with some cool wet towels, placing one on Phil's head. Jenny removed his cooking apron and unbuttoned his shirt. His body felt as hot as the grill and almost as steamy. Jenny sat with Phil's head in her lap wiping the sweat from his neck and arms.

It seemed like an eternity as they waited for the ambulance to arrive. Thoughts raced through Jenny's mind; thoughts of the past and the joys they had shared together, thoughts of their dream to open a restaurant together. Thoughts of what would happen now if Phil was not there to manage the diner they had worked so hard together to establish. It was the first real fear of loneliness Jenny had ever experienced since they met as high school sweethearts.

Another spasm brought Jenny back to the reality at hand.

"Hey!" Steve shouted. "Get some aspirin. I heard it can save a person's life during a heart attack."

Edith rushed to the office and came back with a small bottle of aspirin. She shook a couple into her hand and smashed them a bit with a piece of broken china, and Jenny slid the powder under Phil's tongue. Lisa gave her a glass of water and she drizzled a little into his mouth.

The ambulance had still not arrived.

"Where are they?" Jenny shouted.

"Calm down Jenny, it's only been a couple of minutes," Edith said. "I'll go and meet them and direct them back here."

"You're going to be just fine, Honey Bear. Just hang in there," Jenny whispered to Phil, hope and concern battling for control of her voice. "Just focus on your breathing and hold on."

The soft strains of an ambulance were heard in the distance, then grew sharper, relief piercing the tension of the loyal restaurant patrons who had grown to love the man fighting for his life on the dish room floor. Phil's eyes rolled back into his head, his body becoming lifeless and still.

"Don't you leave me Phil!" Jenny shouted. "Don't you dare leave me! Come on Phil, stay with me!"

A team of paramedics burst into the room where Phil's limp body was cradled in Jenny's arms. Tears streamed down her face, dripping onto Phil's forehead as she looked up at the paramedics, her eyes begging for a miracle, and plead, "Please help."

The paramedics launched into action, checking Phil's vitals, or lack thereof. One began administering CPR. As he pressed the counts on Phil's chest, he said, "Tom, we have a cardiac. I need the defibrillator, stat."

A much younger paramedic came in with a defibrillator and quickly set it up, then began attaching an array of electrodes and wires as the older paramedic prepared to shock Phil's heart.

"Clear!" Tom called, followed by a jolt of power.

The monitor sounded a bleak flatline.

"Clear!" Another jolt was administered, again to no avail. "Okay one more time. Clear!"

That time the miraculous sound of a heartbeat traveled from the monitors to the anxious ears of everyone in the room. Smiles and sighs of relief and gratitude lit their faces as the paramedics continued their work, never missing a beat in their mission to keep Phil alive.

"Tom, get me an IV," the older paramedic called. Within seconds, a solution was going into Phil's arm.

Another siren was closing in from the distance, and then another; police patrol cars this time. The scene outside the diner was a frenzy of black & whites, as if a fellow officer had been shot by a fleeing criminal. City police, county Sheriff's officers and state troopers were crowding both the restaurant and parking lot as Phil was rolled out to the ambulance. The reaction from the officers was no surprise; over the years, Phil had become their favorite cook, even sponsoring three softball teams and a bowling league. Phil was family.

By the time Phil was on his way to the hospital, he had a police escort that rivaled a procession for a fallen officer. At the hospital, doctors rushed to attend to Phil, and the waiting room filled with supporters, everyone eager to encourage Jenny and lift her spirits. As the hours ticked by, however, the loving supporters disappeared one by one back to their duties, leaving Edith and Jenny alone to wait for the prognosis.

…>>…

Phil was startled out of his reminiscent trance by an eager tugging on his arm. Glancing down at a little child with deep red hair and abundant freckles, he quickly scanned the room, only to realize that he was in the office of his restaurant, daydreaming again.

"Grandpa, what'cha thinkin'?" little Mickey asked.

"Oh, sorry Mickey. I was just thinking back to when I had my heart attack. My, that was over 10 years ago. Seems like only yesterday."

"That must-a really hurt Grandpa," Mickey said.

"Oh, yes it did," Phil said, swinging Mickey up in his arms and shooting him to the moon as Mickey squealed joyfully.

Phil turned back to the boxes he was packing, filling each one with one memory after another. Memories of those nights in the hospital, wondering whether he would survive, were as sharp as the culinary knives that had carved out the career to which he had dedicated his life. It was so ironic that those same knives that had carved out his life were also the tools that had almost carved out his death, from the unhealthy foods he was overexposed to.

"Why are you packin'?" Mickey asked.

"Well, we need to go up to our house and stay for a while, and we might need these supplies." Phil said.

"We're goin' to your house?" Mickey said with excitement. "That sounds like fun! I'm gonna go tell Dad we're goin' fishin'!"

Phil wasn't thinking of going fishing, but with a small lake only half a mile away from the house, it actually sounded like a good idea.

"I'm all for it!" Phil laughed as Mickey ran out of the office.

Phil leaned back in his office chair and rested a cool towel on his forehead. There was more concerning him than the anticipated fishing trip to escape the realities of the day, realities Phil didn't want to face. Looking up at the wall of framed pictures, the one of him shaking hands with Dr. Foster at a ceremony stood out among the many. He couldn't help but think back to those many days in the cardiac unit of the hospital, wondering if he would ever be the same.

...<<...

As he lay in his hospital bed, the question kept popping up in his mind: how many people had died in that very same bed? And how many of them could have prevented their early departures? Phil knew that he was, after all, very unhealthy in those days, largely due to the foods he prepared and served at the diner – tasty, but terminal.

The morning after Phil's heart attack, the prognosis from the doctors was grim. As Phil and Jenny listened gravely to the surprising but wise counsel from Dr. Foster, they realized their lives were about to undergo a dramatic change.

"Well Phil, you had a heart attack." Dr. Foster's patients described his dry humor as an acquired taste.

"We sort of figured that out yesterday, Doc," Jenny replied wryly. "What are we doing today? Surgery?"

"We can if you like," Dr. Foster said, pausing at the confused look on their faces. "We can have surgery today, put in a stent, and charge your insurance $60,000. And then I can take a trip to Hawaii for a couple weeks. Or..."

"Or what?" Jenny interrupted. She was exhausted, her nerves were shot, and she was hard pressed to find any humor in the situation.

"Or, we can do something really effective that will change your life forever. Because, quite frankly, I would place all my money on the fact that if you have a stent put in, within another year or two, you will have another heart attack, and then another, and before you know it, you will get the big one that doesn't give you the second chance like you are getting today."

Phil's brow furrowed with concern. "What do you propose, Dr. Foster?" he asked.

"I would like you to change your diet and lifestyle," Dr. Foster replied.

"That's it? Just change my diet?" Phil asked incredulously, looking at Jenny. "I can't tell if he is joking or not."

"Are you serious Doc, do you really just want him to change his diet?" Jenny asked.

Dr. Foster smiled and replied, "Yes, that's it. No pills, no medications, which, by the way, you're going to be on for the rest of your life if you have the surgery, and the pharmaceutical companies are going to love you. At least that's what happens to 95% of the people who have heart surgeries."

"So, you want me to change my diet a little bit… that's fine," Phil agreed.

"A little bit? That's putting it mildly. To say you need to change your diet a little bit is like saying the government is a little bit in debt." The customary twinkle in Dr. Foster's eye quickly dissolved and his expression became solemn. "No. Not just a little, Phil. A lot."

"What is involved in changing his diet 'a lot?'" Jenny asked.

"It means going on a full plant-based diet, with no animal products whatsoever."

"Oh come on! That's not gonna happen. I own a restaurant; I cook meat all day long." Phil said.

"Not just the meat. No cheese, eggs, milk, butter - especially no butter - and no fish."

"What would I eat? Bananas?" Phil asked.

"I'm not monkeying around here, but bananas are great, and lots of them. Plus, you're going to have to eat fruits and vegetables," Dr. Foster said with a look of mock distaste. "And oats and grains too, yuck!" The twinkle was back in his eye.

"Carbs? I'm already overweight, why would I want to eat carbs? I can see cutting back on some of the fatty foods, but eating more starch? That just doesn't make sense. Isn't a 'healthy' diet supposed to eliminate most carbs and focus on protein?"

"Phil, you need to understand that there is a big difference between complex carbs and simple carbs. While we want to stay away from the simple carbs, we *need* the complex carbs. Eat the potato, not the potato chip. The good complex carbs are the wheat, and beans, and rice, and quinoa. Oats are 67% carbs, chickpeas are 27% carbs. Blueberries are 14% carbs, and oranges are 11% carbs. Do you think of those as unhealthy foods?"

"Of course not," Phil replied. "So why is everybody going on these 'no carb' diets?"

"Because of weight loss. Let me give you the secret to

every weight loss diet on the planet."

Phil's ears perked up with genuine curiosity.

"If you eliminate carbs, you will almost certainly lose weight. But if you eliminate sugars, you will lose weight. And if you eliminate oils, you will lose weight. You see, every single diet on the planet has some form of food restriction that translates to calorie restriction, and that's why people lose weight. Even programs like Jenny Craig or Weight Watchers do their calorie restriction through portion control. You simply have to have less calories going into your body than you have burning out in energy. But you see, the people who go on these low-carb Paleo and Atkins diets and the like, end up with some of the highest heart disease rates of all."

"Why don't people know this?" Jenny asked incredulously.

"Well, our culture worships appearance over all else, and everyone wants a 'quick fix.' And to put it bluntly, people are gullible and don't do their homework. We live in a fragmented society, and if you hear something enough times, you will actually believe it, even if it is not true. It's a messed up world, but the statistical facts and the science both show that a plant-based diet is the healthiest on the planet, and we need those carbs."

"The good carbs... the complex ones?"

"Exactly. Listen, Phil, you can get a second opinion. In fact, you can get a dozen other opinions, and every single one of them is going to say 'do the surgery,' and you'll spend the rest of your life fearing the next attack, with a plethora of pills to take every day. Or, you can make a bold move and do something to truly fix this problem rather than putting a bandage on it. You will never regret doing this, but if you go the surgical route, I guarantee you more trouble awaits. This is most likely your last opportunity to get your health to where it should have been all along. Now, I have a full step-by-step program, and I guarantee that if you do exactly what I prescribe, you will have a complete recovery and will feel better than you have in your entire life. But it's going to take a full commitment - your health is so far gone, nothing else will do."

"Can we have a little time to talk about this doctor?" Jenny asked.

"You can talk and pray about it for a day or two. Just remember – you can choose to have surgery and spend weeks here in this hospital bed where many others have died, or you can make the life-changing decision to take charge of your own health. If you do, I will track every step. I would like you to start with a three-week commitment. By then, we will get you serious, life-changing results that you will believe in." As the doctor reached the door of Phil's room he turned back with a wink. "Just so you know, I make a spectacular dairy-free bananas Foster."

"We'll let you know, thanks doctor," Phil chuckled.

"Well, Honey Bear, what do you think?" Jenny asked.

"I think it's extreme, and even he said all the others doctors would agree on the surgery. And look Jenny, this is my life on the line here. Without the surgery, I may not be here another day."

"I think if it was that bad, they would have already done the surgery," Jenny pointed out.

"True," Phil said, "But a plant-based diet… How could I ever do that?"

"I'll help you. I'll do all the cooking," Jenny offered, overlooking Phil's skeptical gaze that implied a lack of confidence in her culinary skill. "You think this dietary change is extreme, but what about open heart surgery? Having a stent put in? Isn't *that* extreme? Look Phil, I don't want to go through this again. Like he said, if you don't listen to him, you're just going to end up back here with another heart attack. Did that heart attack feel good?"

Phil hesitated. "No, it really hurt. It still really hurts."

"Do you want to go through that again?" Jenny pressed.

"No!" Phil replied, this time with conviction.

"Well then, let's pray about it and let Dr. Foster know in the morning."

Phil closed his eyes, clasping Jenny's hands in his and startled her with a prayer unlike anything she had ever heard from this man of little faith.

"Dear Lord in Heaven, give us the direction we need. I don't know what to do. I need Your help. *We* need Your help. I know we haven't exactly been faithful, but we need Your help now. Are You a God that only helps people who are with You when they are not in need, or do You help people who have not really known You, and are pleading for answers? We are expecting great things from You, Lord. We need a miracle. We are anxious to see how You will answer this prayer. Please show us what to do. Amen."

"Amen," Jenny echoed. "I'll go now and let you get some sleep. You have a big decision to make and you need your rest."

As Jenny turned to leave, Phil gripped her hand tightly and whispered, "Tell him we'll do it. After all, I'm a chef. I'm sure I can come up with something good to eat."

Jenny's tear-filled smile said it all as she hurried out excitedly with the good news.

Looking back, Phil contemplated his lifestyle, wondering what was so unhealthy about it. After all, he ate plenty of lean protein and got calcium from an abundance of milk and cheese. That was central to a healthy diet, wasn't it? As a young man, Phil was as strong as an ox, played high school football and ran track, just like every other farm boy in his small town did. But now, gazing down at his obese body, he realized for the first time just how far he had let himself go.

That night, as he lay alone in his hospital room with nothing but the blip of his monitor to break the silence, depression and fear crept in. How could he give up all these foods that he had always considered healthy? Perhaps he should seek a second opinion. After all, Dr. Foster was just one man – a man who had just told him that everything he had ever been taught about nutrition was wrong. Maybe a second opinion offered a way out of the commitment he already regretted making.

Then and Now

Phil awoke as the first shift nurse entered the room, followed by a phlebotomist from the lab department for a blood draw.

"Good morning, Phil. I'm here to get some blood for the lab to test before you eat anything today."

One vial after another was filled. Phil hated these blood draws and had to close his eyes to keep from becoming lightheaded.

"Are you okay Phil?" the technician asked. "We're almost done."

"That's a lot of blood. Why so many vials?" Phil asked.

Handing Phil some orange juice, the nurse replied; "The doctor wants to cover all the bases and get a good perspective of what may be going on."

Just then Jenny walked in and hesitated, startled by the presence of the others in the room.

"I'm just finishing up here," the phlebotomist said. "Keep an eye on him, we drew a lot of blood."

"A lot of blood?" Phil questioned with an attitude. "No honey, they drew a LOT of blood. She's like a vampire. I bet you're not even human."

The phlebotomist tossed him a wickedly funny look, "And my boss's name is Dracula."

Phil hissed good-naturedly as the technician left the room

laughing.

"Well, your humor is still there, even if your blood isn't." Jenny greeted him, planting a kiss on his forehead.

"Yeah, that was rough. I've never had anyone take that much blood," Phil replied. "So, who's working the shop?"

"Steve's in there this morning," Jenny said. "You know there's nowhere else he would be right now; he's beside himself with worry over you. Also, a young man came in yesterday after hearing about your heart attack and said he could help out. He came back first thing this morning as Steve and I were arriving."

"Did he have brown hair?" Phil asked.

"Yes."

"Was his face a little scruffy and unshaven?"

"Yes."

"Wearing a light brown jacket?"

"Yes, I believe he was. How did you know?" Jenny asked curiously.

"Jenny, you are not going to believe this. I had a dream last night that I was talking to 'The Master Chef' and He was going to send me a helper."

"The Master Chef? Well, Mike - his name is Mike - is a chef. At least, I think he is. And he did say something about working for a Master Chef."

"Yes! I saw this man in a vision," Phil said with conviction.

"This is too weird."

"Do you really think these things are connected?" Jenny asked.

"How could they not be? He said he would change our diet, change our health... change our lives." Phil seemed lost in thought for a moment, then added, "I wonder if this is our answer to prayer."

"Well, it could just be a coincidence, but he did say he was kind of a health nut," Jenny added. "Was his name Mike in your dream?"

"I didn't get a name," Phil responded.

"Well, that's his name, and I hired him today. He'll be starting Monday morning." Jenny paused to wait for Phil's reaction.

"I wonder what all this means?" Phil questioned, "It was such a clear and vivid vision."

"Or, just a dream." Jenny's skepticism kicked in. "Whatever it was, the bottom line is that you are going to have to deal with a new person in the kitchen. We need the help. Doctor Foster says you're not going to be sweating over the grill for quite some time."

"I don't know how in the world we can afford to hire somebody; we are barely making the bills now."

"Trust in the Lord; I'm sure He has a plan for us," Jenny said reassuringly, giving Phil the look of gentle comfort that he had come to rely on so much over the years.

Jenny put her arms around Phil and wouldn't let go. She

knew that this was a step long overdue for the hard-working man she loved so much. Kitchen work is strenuous and demanding, and many years had been spent working at what seemed to be an endless cycle of budget verses growth. But Jenny's faith was being renewed, sparked by God's grace in this second chance.

Dr. Foster entered the room with a tray full of food. "Hello and good morning! I thought I might take the liberty of bringing you the first breakfast of your healthy transformation."

"Morning, Doc!" Phil said.

"Wow, look at all this food!" Jenny gasped.

"And you are going to eat every bite of it," Dr. Foster demanded.

"Oh no! I just can't eat this early in the morning," Phil said.

"It's 9:30 Phil. What time do you normally get to work?" Dr. Foster asked.

"It's always different, depending on what shifts I'm covering," Phil replied.

"Two things we are going to have to deal with right now are sleep times and meal times," Dr. Foster stated. "We need consistency."

"Phil is more of an early bird, and I generally stay up later," Jenny said.

"Perfect. What time does the restaurant open?" Dr. Foster inquired.

"Six in the morning," Jenny said.

"And you probably get there at what, five?" Dr. Foster asked.

"Yes," Phil responded. "I do have an opener. But if I have to open, that's when I'm there."

"That means you will have to be in bed at eight o'clock every night."

"You can't be serious! No, no, no, we don't even close till seven p.m.!" Phil exclaimed with all the force he could muster.

"Do you have a closer? Like you have an opener?" Dr. Foster asked.

"Yes, but you never know if we'll have a catered event. It just doesn't work that way in the restaurant business," Jenny responded.

"I admit I don't know a lot about the restaurant business," Dr. Foster replied. "But, I do know the necessity of getting you in a healthy pattern so you don't end up with a fatal heart attack two weeks from now. Are we clear on this? You have got to get the time management in order."

"Phil, I'll do the closing at night if need be," Jenny volunteered. "And as far as the catering, you do the prep in the daytime, and I'll work with the team to close it down."

"So bed at eight every night," Dr. foster continued. "Wake up time is four a.m. I'll even give you a little wiggle room from 9:00 p.m. to 5:00 a.m. But that's it."

"Okay, boss - I mean doc," Phil answered with a depressed chuckle.

"That's good, you just think of me as your boss for the next 50 years," Dr. Foster quipped back. "Now, about your eating habits; we need you to have a big breakfast, a smaller lunch, and an even smaller dinner."

"This is just too much food, Doc," Phil said.

"It is today, but after a couple days of having a very small dinner, you will be ready for a big breakfast every morning. Remember, we have to do some drastic things to reverse all that damage that has been done over the last few decades. So get to work on that breakfast!"

As Phil began to eat, his cringing frown turned into a pleased smile. "This is actually pretty good oatmeal," Phil commented.

"One of my secret recipes," Dr. Foster said with a wink.

"I thought you said he couldn't have any milk," Jenny commented, looking over the tray.

"It's almond milk," Dr. Foster replied. "Dairy free. And you will notice all the starches - whole grain bread, oatmeal, and a biscuit. I want you to eat all your heavy carbohydrates in the morning, as they are going to burn off throughout the day. Salads for lunch, every day. Dinners will be small, maybe just veggies with brown rice." Pulling a thin booklet out of his pocket, the doctor added, "Here is a menu for an entire month. It's simple and easy-to-follow and in a couple months, we will show you how to tweak it for some variety that you are going to love."

Skimming through the book, Jenny commented,

"Pancakes, fruit, breads, rice, potatoes; these are a lot of the things we carry at the restaurant. This doesn't look that tough."

"It's not," Dr. Foster added. "But you have to understand that it's how you prepare the food that really matters. You can take a perfectly good potato and kill it with a ton of butter. You can't add a pound of sugar to your granola. After a couple weeks of consistent simplicity, your taste buds will start doing the job they're supposed to be doing, and you will be craving the healthier options. Just you wait and see."

"Well, when can we go home and get started?" Jenny asked.

"Give me three more days here," Dr. Foster hesitated, "Then we will run a heart stress test, and after that we should have you home in no time at all. There's no way your heart is in good enough shape to do anything right now. It just needs rest."

"Not exactly what I had in mind for a vacation, but I do feel burned out and totally exhausted," Phil said.

"And rest you shall have. Just eat everything on the plates we send you, *when* we send them to you," Dr. Foster said firmly. "Remember, *when* you eat is almost as important as *what* you eat. I will also have another blood test in a couple days. Just a single vial this time," he added to Phil's relief. "Then we'll see you after the test results are in."

"Well that's good, because I don't think I have any blood left after this morning," Phil replied ruefully.

"If you need anything, just call," Dr. Foster called over his shoulder as he exited the room to continue his morning rounds. "My office is connected to the hospital."

"Thanks, Doc," Jenny replied, waving after him.

Phil was ready for a nap, so Jenny headed over to the restaurant to help hold the fort in the absence of their leader.

…>>…

Phil awoke to a tap on the door, only to find himself back at the restaurant leaning back in his office chair. Startled from his memories of days gone by, he looked up from his reverie to see Steve entering the room.

"Sorry Captain, just looking for little Mickey," Steve said.

"Oh, hi Steve. Mickey was here a minute ago; he's probably in the back prep line with Eddie. I think he's cooking me breakfast."

"He just can't get enough of the kitchen," Steve said.

"At seven years old, I think we have the youngest chef on the planet," Phil chuckled.

"And he's actually really good too!" Steve couldn't quite manage to hide the pride in his voice.

"I noticed. That little Mickey really takes after his father," Phil remarked.
"He had a good teacher."

"But he sure doesn't take after you when it comes to looks!" Jenny said, coming through the door. "I mean look at you - sandy brown hair, no freckles."

"I'm stockier built too," Steve added. "Yeah, he really does look like his mother. So, are you ready for our walk?" Steve asked.

"Yes, but just look at this, you two." Phil couldn't wait to show Steve those horrible test results from over a decade ago. "Cholesterol at 970, triglycerides at 341, HDL down at 27, and LDL at 221 - these were horrible, just horrible!"

"I can't believe you were ever in such bad shape." Steve said, humoring the notion for the 20th time. "How much weight did you lose?"

"Over 150 pounds now," Phil exclaimed. "I was about 375 pounds at the time of the heart attack. Now I'm hanging in around 225."

"Wow! Well, let me take a walk around and find out where your breakfast is and then we can get moving."

"Mickey!" Steve set off in search of his son, finding him in the kitchen preparing his honorary grandpa's oatmeal.

"I don't know what you would do without Steve." Jenny said.

"He really has stepped up to the plate over the last few years," Phil said.
"And to think, when I brought him on, he was just a troubled kid in need of some structure, discipline and fatherly care. He started out as a bus boy – a bad one at that – and now he's running the entire restaurant!"

Jenny smiled, remembering Steve as a struggling teenager. "Mick would be so proud of him today – and of you, for taking him on like that."

"It was the least I could do. Mick was my best friend. He always did so much for everyone else. The least I could do was step in and help his boy when he needed it. Losing his dad turned Steve's life upside down. Poor Ellen had her hands full just trying to keep a roof over their heads. She wasn't prepared to deal with an angry teenage boy acting out in his grief." Phil's eyes welled up a bit at the memory of his best friend and the difficult years after his death.

"Well, it turned out to be a blessing for both Steve and you. You were there for him, and now he's here for you."

Phil smiled. "He's the son I never had. I can't imagine life without him now, or little Mickey."

Just then, the door opened and Mickey proudly carried in a breakfast tray fit for a king, beaming as he received his grandpa's hug of appreciation and praise for a job well done. After breakfast, Steve and Phil headed out for their morning walk.

As they walked, Phil thought of just how valuable Steve had become to him since the heart attack. "You are so in tune with this restaurant; I couldn't be more pleased with how you have taken over the lead operating position."

Steve smiled humbly. "Well, I had a good teacher."

"We all had a good teacher," Phil said, "But it's the action you took applying what we have learned and putting it into practice that makes me so proud of you. You're a real asset, son."

"Thank you, I'm glad I can help," Steve replied. Eager to take the focus off of himself, he asked, "So, have you been enjoying your new trailer?"

"We've only taken it out twice, but yeah; it's so nice to get into the wilderness and really draw closer to the Lord."

"One of these days, I'm going to have to talk you into letting me take it for the weekend," Steve suggested.

"Anytime son. My house is your house. How long have you been working with me now?" Phil asked.

"20 some years," Steve responded.

"And Lisa has been with us for 14 years," Phil said. "I sure do love her."

"Me too. That's why I married her," Steve said with a grin. "The only one who's been here longer is Edith."

"Edith…" Phil worked out the dates in his head. "25 years! Who would have thought. And she is just the sweetest little old lady."

"She was old 20 years ago, bless her heart," Steve said.

"Yeah, but what a trooper," Phil added. "She could handle more tables than anyone I've ever met. Really saved our business in those early years when we couldn't even afford the mortgage, let alone pay wages."

"And look at her now," Steve commented. "Still sharp as a tack. A bit slower, but she doesn't miss a trick."

"And what a godly woman." Phil added, "I'm so glad you've got her in the hostessing position now. I know she loves it too. The body can only take so much of these hard restaurant years."

"Yeah, just look at you, Mr. Heart Attack," Steve reflected.

"Thank God we are working smarter now. My stress levels

are nothing compared to what they were then," Phil said.

"Oh by the way, I found that generator you wanted," Steve said. "They will be delivering it to the house next week, along with a five-hundred gallon gas tank."

"Good, we'll put that right behind the barn," Phil said.

"Seems like a lot of gas; do you really need that much?" Steve questioned.

"Well that's what I was advised to get. If the power goes out again like it did last winter, I'm going to be covered," Phil said. "You're okay here in town, but out where we are, it took them a whole week to get the power restored."

"And we know that someday you may need it for other reasons," Steve pointed out. Phil nodded solemnly.

Steve went back to work in the kitchen while Phil went to his office for his usual morning siesta. Kicking back on his reclining couch, Phil pondered why he had invested in such a big generator. One thing he knew for certain was that it was for a purpose greater than the foreseeable needs of the restaurant.

…<<…

As Phil rested, his thoughts traveled back to those days of obesity and fear in the cardiac unit. A knock on the hospital room door startled Phil from his midmorning rest, and a young man entered with a humbly curious look.

"Good morning. Are you Phil?" the young man asked.

"Yes, and I would guess that you're Mike?" Phil replied.

"Yes, I am. How did you know?" Mike asked.

"I have friends in high places. Plus, my wife told me about you." Phil kept his tone a bit guarded as he tried to decide what to make of this mysterious yet familiar young man.

"Well I'm sorry to bother you, but I just felt the need to talk before I start working for you."

"I appreciate that," Phil said.

"Yeah, well, if it were me, I would want to meet me first." Mike smiled.

"So, you're a chef?" Phil knew that chefs could be a real pain. Never having pursued a culinary degree himself, his education came from the school of hard knocks.

"Well, I'm more of a servant. I've worked for master chefs. What are your needs right now?" Mike asked.

"Well right now, the doctor says I need to get healthy," Phil grinned, grabbing his spare tire with both hands. "We have a couple line cooks, but they're not that good, and they're both going to school, so I only get them part-time. I generally spend a lot of time on the line. Steve is just a prep assistant with very little knowledge of food, but he is a good listener and does what you say. We've got our dishwashers, Eddie and Eric. They're a couple of Mexican brothers; young, but good-hearted boys. They're good workers, and you will love them. Plenty of good servers, and Jenny can take care of the front of the house. But for the kitchen, I need a producer. I need someone who can get the prep work done efficiently and watch that front line."

"I can do that," Mike said confidently, then hesitated for a second. "But I need to be straight with you right up front - I don't work on Saturdays."

"You don't work Saturdays? Why, that's one of our busiest days! Why can't you work Saturdays?" Phil asked, beginning to doubt this providential help just a little.

"That's the Sabbath. Sunset Friday to sunset Saturday," Mike replied.

"You mean the Jewish Sabbath? Are you Jewish?" Phil asked.

"I'm a Christian, and I simply follow what the Bible says," Mike said, his tone gentle but full of conviction.

"The Bible says that Saturday is the Sabbath, not Sunday?" Phil asked incredulously.

"Yes sir, it does. The seventh-day Sabbath is Saturday, always has been and always will be, according to the Bible. But I'll tell you what," Mike offered, "I'll do double prep on Fridays, so there will be plenty of everything to get through the weekend."

"And you'll work Sundays?" Phil asked.

"Yes Sir," Mike agreed.

"Well, Sundays are the toughest day to get people to work. That's church day here in the Bible belt, and we get busy with a lot of big tops." Thinking deeply, Phil asked, "Are you *sure* Saturday is really the Sabbath?"

"Yes, Sir," Mike replied again.

"Then how is it that everyone is going to church on Sunday?" Phil asked with genuine curiosity.

"Well, not everyone. There are millions of people who know that God has set aside Saturday as holy. Unfortunately, Satan has ways of twisting things, and the truth has been covered up over generations."

Phil wasn't sure what to make of this strange new information, and he was too exhausted to put much thought into it now, but he believed Mike to be an honest guy. His request for Saturdays off seemed fair enough, especially since he was willing to work Sundays. Phil could see the young man wasn't lazy, just a little strange in his beliefs, but he could work with that.

"Well, I'll give you Saturdays off if you'll be my opener in the mornings," Phil counter-offered. "And take a couple half-days off so I can have you six mornings a week."

"I can do that." Mike smiled, holding out his hand to shake on the deal.

"What about the wages?" Phil asked. He needed to know if he could even afford Mike's help before confirming his acceptance.

"I don't want to know," Mike replied. "Don't even know what good wages are around here. Pay me what you think is fair and I'll be happy." Phil almost couldn't believe it – this seemed too good to be true. Perhaps this was the Lord's doing, after all, he thought, and slowly raised his hand to shake on the agreement.

"Great! Get together with Steve. He knows his way around and will be happy to get you acclimated to the kitchen. Have Jenny show you the books for ordering. A man named Sam will be there Tuesday morning to get a food order from you. The deliveries come on Wednesdays. We get food from three different suppliers, and all that info is in the binder."

Minutes ticked by into hours as the two of them went over the finer points of the restaurant and its day-to-day operations, with Phil conveying to Mike the minutest details that made up the heartbeat of this struggling little cafe. Everything from where light switches were located, to the directions for particular recipes. Phil had a passion for his livelihood, and his concerns were reflected in the seriousness of his explanations.

As Mike was absorbing the challenge, he would ask one good question after another, and in no time at all, Phil had a sense that Mike would work out well for the restaurant.

When Mike asked, "Can I pray with you?" Phil wasn't surprised as he immediately agreed. They bowed their heads as Mike prayed, "Father in heaven, we thank You for this day that You have given us. We humble ourselves before Your throne and ask You to be with Phil in his healing process; give him the determination of transformation that can only come from You. Help us, Lord, with the work at hand, so we can experience the full fruits of Your prosperity in the business You have provided. Teach us how to set ourselves aside and accomplish more with Your hands working through us. We pray these words, knowing that You answer prayer, that You ARE our answer to prayer. Amen."

"Amen." Phil grasped Mike's hand and said with all sincerity, "Thank you."

"You just get better, and we'll see you in a few weeks."

As Mike left, Phil sighed in relief, free from the stress of wondering how he would manage the restaurant. He soon drifted off into the first peaceful sleep he'd had in a very long time.

Welcome Back

With the stress tests in hand, Dr. Foster entered Phil's hospital room to discuss his results.

"Good morning, Phil. How are you feeling?"

"Much better, doc," Phil replied. "When am I going to get out of here?"

"Just as soon as we go over these test results." Dr. Foster's gaze zoomed in on Phil's eyes. "Hmmm," He said. "That's good."

"What's good?" Phil asked. "What do my eyes have to do with anything?"

"Your eyes can tell a lot. In fact, when you first came here, the outer edge of your iris was rather fuzzy, and now it is much sharper. And that's really good." Touching Phil's skin, Dr. Foster continued. "Your cells are reacting much faster too, with better color." Slapping Phil's arm, he noted, "It's red. That means you're getting more oxygen into the blood stream, which is excellent."

"And what about the test results?" Phil asked.

"Impressive." Dr. Foster replied, turning the chart toward Phil and showing him the high points. "See, your cholesterol is now at 425. Dropped over 500 points with no statins whatsoever. Just diet alone! And not even exercising."

"That's amazing!" Phil stammered in utter surprise.

"What does concern me, though…" the doctor paused, his brow furrowing as he analyzed the numbers on the chart in his hand, "your LDL is still too high, and your HDL is way too low. It's still too risky to send you out on your own yet."

"Come on, Doc," Phil pleaded, "I've gotta get out of here!"

"There's that anxiety I'm concerned about," Dr. Foster explained. "Can you feel your heart racing? Blood pressure rising?"

"Yes," Phil said quietly, knowing the doctor was right without even checking his vitals.

"Look Phil," Dr. Foster said with all seriousness, "I'll let you out of here as long as you promise me you will stay at home for the next three weeks without stepping one foot into the restaurant."

"Doc?" Phil exclaimed, hoping for a sympathetic reprieve.

"*And...*" Dr. Foster continued, unmoved, "you promise to take 3 walks a day, five to fifteen minutes each.

"Okay, I promise."

"Wait a second," Dr. Foster said. Searching his pockets, he pulled out a recorder for his notes and, pressing the record button, asked, "What was that, Phil?"

"Okay, okay. I promise I'll stay at home." Phil said, chuckling resignedly.

"Great!" Dr. Foster smiled. Then, sobering up, he continued, "The reason I say this is because 30% of people who have a heart attack have another attack within the first couple of weeks after. And 80% of those are fatal. After what you've been through, your heart can't handle another."

"I hear you Doc," Phil said. "I know I'm in good hands."

"You're in the hands of someone more powerful than me," Dr. Foster said, pointing upward. "Healing from years of damage doesn't happen overnight, but if you take the right steps, there is no reason why you can't have a total recovery and enjoy that healthy body you should have had all along."

"Thanks, Doc."

"I'll be calling you every week, and I'll stay in touch with Jenny, too. In fact, I'll go call her right now and let her know to get you an escort out of here." Dr. Foster clapped Phil on the shoulder and tossed a copy of the test results on the bed as he walked out the door. "Great first week, great results!"

Phil's smile was ear-to-ear. He wasn't sure if it was more because of the test results, or getting out of that dreadful hospital. Either way, he was thankful.

After three weeks of home confinement, Phil felt like a new man. His walks were up to fifteen minutes at a time and his breathing was much better, too. There was still no way he was going to be able to jump right into the kitchen, but the restaurant was his life, and not Jenny nor Dr. Foster were going to keep him away another second.

The whole restaurant cheered as Phil walked in the door. He smiled as he read the banner over the register: "Welcome back Phil... Now get back to work!"

As he waded through the crowd of well-wishers, the many tearful hugs, kisses and handshakes reminded Phil that these people were less like employees and more like family.

It seemed like every softball team in the league and at least half the police force was there. Jack, the police chief, shouted as he grabbed Phil's belly. "If this is what happens to the people that eat here, I'm putting the entire force on restriction!" The crowd laughed and booed as he said, "No more eating at Phil's!"

One by one, each person said hello and welcomed Phil back. The excitement of the crowd, as kind as they had been, began to take a noticeable toll on Phil's stress level, and everyone realized it was time to go.

As the crowd began to dissipate, Phil noticed Mike in the kitchen prepping. Phil made his way through the main line, then the coolers, and couldn't believe how organized they were. Everything was clearly labeled, sparkling clean, and looked fresh. It was like walking into a whole new kitchen. Mike glanced up at Phil, waiting for an appraisal as Phil methodically scrutinized every nook and cranny.

Finally, Phil approached Mike and offered his sincerest praise. "This place really looks good."

"Thank you, Captain," Mike replied, smiling humbly.

"I can't believe you did all this in just four weeks!"

"Well sir, it really didn't take all that long, and the team adapted quite easily. They were a little skeptical at first, but that didn't last long." Mike leaned in and whispered, "I think they're working harder, too."

Phil smiled and said with deep gratitude, "Thank you, Mike."

"My pleasure. And when you find some time over the next couple weeks, I would like to go over a few things that I couldn't do without you."

"That will be fine," Phil responded.

After socializing with a few of the employees that were still there, Jenny grabbed Phil's hand and said, "Come with me to the office."

Phil raised his eyebrows quizzically, but Jenny just grinned and said "come on!" as she led him back to the office, which also served as a makeshift break room and catch-all.

Phil stared in disbelief at the transformed room, with a fresh coat of paint and new artwork on the walls. A large desk and filing cabinets anchored the room, with space enough on the left for a sofa, recliner, and coffee table. Behind the desk was a counter, and above it hung a large framed cork board with a row of 8 clipboards, designed for specific tasks.

"Did Mike do this too?" Phil asked, amazed.

"We both did," Jenny replied, carefully gauging his reaction.

"Don't you think this is a little out of his boundary as an employee?"

"I thought you might react this way, feeling like you were being usurped a little. And with any other man, I would agree, but Mike is a good man, and a real blessing to have here. Give him a chance to explain himself, and you will understand. He's been working night and day making this place look good for you, and I think he deserves a bonus."

Phil continued to gaze around the room, taking it all in. "I never realized this room was so big."

"Neither did I," Jenny replied. "And look at this." Jenny walked over to the left wall, where a curtain hung about four feet from the floor. She drew back the curtain, revealing a smoked glass window about four feet long and two feet high. Through the window, the majority of the restaurant's exterior and front entrance could be seen.

Phil immediately went out to the front of the restaurant to see what the other side of the window looked like. It was a framed, etched glass mirror that no one would ever suspect was a window. He leaned in close to check if he could see through the window. The only way he could get a glimpse was with his eyes less than an inch away and his hands covering the glare.

As he walked back to the office, Phil stuck his head in the kitchen and asked Mike, "Do you have a little time right now, or should we talk later?"

"Sure, Captain, now is fine."

Jenny fidgeted nervously as they entered the office, wondering if Phil was pleased or mad about the changes. Did he consider them a blessing, or a pride-wounding challenge to his authority?

Once they were seated, Phil leaned back in his chair, his face inscrutable.

"You did all of this, Mike?" Phil said, concern in his voice.

"Yes sir, and then some."

"And then some? What else don't I know about?" Phil looked pointedly at Jenny, who carefully avoided his gaze.

"Well, I have a lot of things I want to walk you through."

"That's fine, but the first thing I want to know is, where did the money come from to do all of this?"

Jenny and Mike glanced at each other conspiratorially. It was time to reveal the secrets that Jenny had been keeping from Phil for the last three weeks. Since Jenny had been the one to approve the purchases, she felt she should do the explaining.

"Almost everything came from thrift stores, so the cost was relatively minimal," Jenny said.

"How much was this rug?" Phil asked, pointing down at the beautiful wool rug that centered the desk.

"Um, I think it was $20.00," Mike said.

"No," Jenny corrected. "The desk was $20.00; the rug was $25.00."

"I stand corrected. It was $25.00," Mike said, grinning. "Phil, how do you like your new $10.00 office chair?"

As Phil looked down at the chair beneath him in wonder, he tried to maintain his composure, but was overwhelmed with joyful gratitude. His lips trembled slightly as he spoke, and a tear escaped the corner of his eye and slid down his cheek. "I am so thankful. I wish you wouldn't have spent the money on me, but this is an absolute blessing. Thank you both so very much."

Jenny was at Phil's side in an instant, wrapping him in a giant hug, tossing Mike a wink and a thumbs-up behind Phil's back.

"Check this out Phil," Mike pointed through the window.

"I designed the height of this window so you have a bird's-eye view from your desk. You can spend more time back here taking it easy, but still see all the activity and who is coming and going in the restaurant."

Phil's smile said it all.

Mike continued. "As far as the money goes, the first week, our food costs were at 47%. The second week we were at 42%, and this last week we hit 39%. I think I can get you down to 35% and, if we redesign your menu, I can definitely get you down to 25%, maybe even 23%."

"Who are you?" Phil said with an incredulous laugh. "Is there anything you can't do?"

Mike chuckled. "God has gifted me with talents, just like He has gifted you. And now, you are both going from having to work day and night in the trenches to the leadership roles that He wants you to take." As Mike pointed toward the sky, he continued. "He has big plans for you. Your restaurant is a diamond in the rough. With the savings you'll have on food costs, you can hire three more employees, *or* close for the Sabbath and still be fine." Mike smiled, rapidly raising and lowering his brows, fishing for a green light from Phil.

"One step at a time here, Mike," Phil said good-naturedly. Let's look at the functionality first, though I do like the thought of a menu redesign. Let's start working on that."

"Yes sir, and I do apologize for taking such drastic measures while you were out. Most people would never give me the opportunity to implement the vision because they are so focused on the now, and not the future. With you in the hospital, this was a perfect opportunity to do it."

"You're right," Phil agreed, "I would never have approved

of any of this. But it works; it just works. Thank you again, Mike."

"Thank you, Captain. But I'd better get back to work; I have a lunch to get prepped."

Mike hurried from the room, leaving Jenny and Phil locked in a gaze.

"39%?" Phil asked, dumbfounded.

"Yes, and I was the one double-checking it," Jenny replied.

"We need to keep this young man around."

"Absolutely." Jenny answered with conviction. "He is the humblest and pleasant person to be around. And he produces! Wait until you see him in the kitchen. I've never seen anybody who could move so fast and stay so calm."

"He hasn't asked for more money?" Phil asked.

"No, but if I were you, I would add another couple bucks an hour to his wages."

"You're right. Let's take him out for dinner next weekend, too."

Jenny gave Mike another big hug, and the two of them sat for a while at the picture frame window, looking into the restaurant.

The Master Chef

Mike was hard at work when Phil showed up the next morning. There was a relaxed atmosphere in the kitchen, not the normal chaos that Phil was accustomed to.

"Give me five minutes and I'll have your breakfast ready," Mike called out cheerfully.

"No thanks Mike, I'm fine," Phil said.

"Did you eat?" Mike asked.

"No," Phil replied. I'm not a big breakfast person."

"That was then, and this is now," Mike said. "You are to eat a big breakfast every day, doctor's orders. So get in your office and start going through your inbox. You have weeks of catching up to do and your future is waiting."

Phil nodded in agreement as he headed to his office. Walking by the front line, he expected to see Steve and one of the boys, but there was no Steve, only Eddie and Eric, the dishwashers. Lisa was waiting for her order to come to the window.

Phil whispered to Lisa, "How are those two doing back there?"

"Great, Boss. They're fast, consistent and the food looks good," Lisa responded.

Phil took a look at the plates coming through the window and sure enough, they looked fantastic, embellished with a twisted orange garnish on a red kale flower. The aroma of fresh pancakes filled the air, and he could tell they had used a different recipe. Looking at the two youngsters with a smile, Phil commented, "You guys are doing great back there."

"Thank you, Captain," they responded.

Phil couldn't help but snoop around a bit, opening drawers and peeking in cupboards, and he was pleased to see such a clean and organized servers' station. Continuing to his office, he found a bowl of oatmeal and a couple of slices of rye toast waiting for him. He wondered how it got there without him seeing anyone put it there. Mike entered with some fresh fruit and raw mixed nuts.

"Now, make sure you eat it all and then we can take a walk while we strategize about what direction we're going." Mike rushed out of the room as if there was something boiling over on the stove, leaving Phil to enjoy the service and the sense of peace in his new office.

Phil was beginning to feel a little uneasy. He wasn't sweating over the grill, he wasn't rushing the lunch specials, he was just sitting in his new office all alone, and it didn't feel right. He was a hard-working man who was used to hands-on management and being the one to get things done. Now he could only stand back and watch as his business operated without him.

After breakfast, Phil noticed the restaurant did not appear nearly as busy as usual. Wondering where the usual customers were, and the volume of business that reflected years of service, Phil had a major concern.

"Are you ready, Captain?" Mike appeared at the door.

"Ready for what?" replied Phil.

"It's time to walk and talk." Mike took Phil by the arm and

with both hands, gently steered Phil out of the building. Phil hesitated as he looked around, expecting the 7:00 am rush hour. He couldn't help looking worried as he glanced at his watch as he asked, "Are you sure they can handle it?"

"Don't worry, they're doing great. We're still training, but they have the fundamentals down quite well. You must have given them some great foundational experience, because they really do good work."

Walking down the dirt road behind the restaurant, Phil was uneasy. "I'm really concerned, Mike. It's rush hour."

"Well then, we'd better walk quicker." Mike replied with a laugh.
"And why is the place so slow this morning?" Phil asked. "I'm really concerned about that too."

Mike smiled reassuringly and explained, "Well, it may appear as though there are fewer customers, because there isn't a backlog. In reality, we are just quicker, turning the same number of tables twice as fast as we did the first week. Your ticket time in the kitchen for breakfast was 10 to 12 minutes when I first arrived, and now they are running 6 to 8 minutes, with a lot of tables having less than a 5-minute ticket turn."

"Really? How is that possible?" Phil asked.

"It's all about the prep; being ready for the order before it happens. In fact, right now the servers have to drop the toast in the toaster as soon as they place the order, because some of the orders come out before the toast is done."

"And these guys in the kitchen can handle that?" Phil asked.

"Sure, it's breakfast. A no-brainer. That's why we're bringing Steve in later in the day. These kids can handle the morning."

Walking a little farther, it became obvious that Phil was getting winded and Mike knew he couldn't push him too hard, even though it was just ten minutes.

"You really need to get more walking in," Mike said as they stopped on a bridge.

"Well, I'm game for a walk like this every day if you are." Phil replied, his chest heaving a bit from the exertion.

"Sure thing, Captain," Mike assured him. "I'll help you follow the doctor's orders."

On their walk back, Phil remembered his dream in the hospital weeks before. Was this a coincidence or an actual, sent-from-heaven helper?

Trying to be discreet, Phil decided to probe in a roundabout way.
"So tell me Mike, where did you get all this culinary knowledge?" Phil asked.

"Well, I grew up cooking in the kitchen," Mike replied.

"Was your family in the business?"

"No. We lived in a tourist area, where they would hire anybody. I was bussing tables at ten years old and washing dishes when I was eleven. By the time I was twelve, my brothers and I were working the main line, cooking."

"Yeah, but you don't learn what you've learned just by growing up that way. Where did you go to school?" Phil persisted.

"Cooking school?" Mike asked. In response to Phil's nod, he continued, "I never went to a culinary arts school."

"Come on, you must have had some kind of training."

"No, none."

"None?" Phil asked, incredulous. "Who did you work under?"

"No one. Once I learned how to cook, things just took off. Everywhere I have ever been, I was hired as the lead."

"Well, you're the best I've ever seen," Phil said. "And I've only seen a little of your talent."

"Please understand, I'm not bragging," explained Mike. "God has gifted me with a talent, and I've always sought to make the most of it. Because of that, He has blessed me, and I've been able to offer the places I've worked much more than they've previously experienced."

"It's way beyond what I've ever seen, I'll tell you that," Phil added, "I mean, you are just so fast and organized. It really blows me away. The rest of the team, too. It's like they know that they are privileged to work with such talent. Is that why they are so willing to do what you ask of them?"

"I don't know about that. I just give them a vision of what they can be," Mike replied. "Don't you have a vision? A goal?"

Contemplating his own aspirations, Phil said, "I've worked hard to get where we are today, but I have really been struggling so much just trying to stay afloat, that we really haven't looked that far ahead. I mean, we have desires, but not really a plan."

"And now with your condition, you are going to have to work smarter and leave the manual labor up to us." Mike said.

"You really are gifted, you should be on television or something. Or running some huge place in Vegas. Celebrities would give their right arm for talent like yours." Phil mentioned.

Mike grinned. "No one's ever given me a limb, but many celebrities have enjoyed my work and paid me well for it.

"Really? Where? Have you worked in Vegas?" Phil asked. Without waiting for the answer, he continued, "You have, haven't you?"

Mike nodded in confirmation.

"Wow, I've always wanted to go there. Where did you work?"

"My last job was as the Executive Chef at the Tropicana."

"WHAT? You're kidding me!"

"No, I'm not. Actually, I've been an executive chef at seven different casinos. I was also a food and beverage director for the Golden Nugget, running both of their properties in Vegas and in Laughlin, Nevada."

"Wait, that's a lot of experience, and you're still pretty young. When did you start running the show like that?"

"I got my first job as an executive chef in a Vegas casino

at the age of 24. I was the youngest executive chef of any casino there. Before that, I ran smaller casinos in various parts of Nevada."

"Amazing."

"It was quite a wild ride…" Mike's voice trailed off and he seemed lost in the past for a moment.

"So what celebrities did you work with? Give me some names," Phil pleaded, undisguised excitement in his tone.

Mike snapped back to the present with a chuckle. "I don't even know where to start. Umm… Rock stars like Madonna, the Rolling Stones, and Aerosmith. Actors like Halle Barry, Meryl Streep, and John Travolta. Politicians like Harry Reid, Mike Huckabee, and President Carter." Mike blushed a bit, uncomfortable with name-dropping, and not wanting to sound boastful.

"You catered for President Carter?"

"I've done many events for him. Of course, this was years after he was president. I'm not that old!"

"What did you do for him?" Phil continued probing.

"I helped with several of his humanitarian projects. He came in and out of Vegas and sometimes he flew me to various places around the world, organizing his events. Every couple years or so he calls me to get a team together." Mike checked his watch, eager to change the subject. "Which reminds me, we'd better go check on *your* team before it really does get busy."

"Good idea. You know, I really can't believe that someone with your level of experience, who has worked with some of the biggest names in entertainment and politics is here, managing my little small-town diner. How could you leave such an exciting life behind?"

Mike's voice became serious. "Don't let the glamorous exterior of celebrity life fool you, Phil. I made that mistake when I was younger, and I regret it. I know better now. To answer your question, it wasn't hard to leave. My life belongs to God, so I follow where He leads. I'm here with you now because this is where God wants me to be."

Mike changed the subject as they crossed back over the bridge and headed toward the restaurant. "I've got a question for you. You thought it was slow in there, even though we are turning more tables than ever before. Do you suppose people will think business has dropped off because they're not waiting in line for 20 minutes anymore?"

"I don't think so," Phil replied. "We'll probably get a better reputation, attracting even more repeat customers with our faster service."

"That reminds me of when I first got started running casinos. I was working for a little casino in Henderson, Nevada. My first day on the job, the owner said, 'I've got a line out the door, what in the world is going on in here?' I had two egg pans in each hand at the time, and I flipped all four sets of eggs in one motion and explained to him, 'John, I can feed every one of these people in three minutes flat, but if I do, they won't be out there filling your slot machines.' He looked out at the busy casino floor and realized how much more business was actually going on. He never questioned me again. Now that he believed I knew what I was doing, I knew I could offer more suggestions to help his business, so I asked, 'John, why are we giving back dimes at the cash registers? We don't have any dime slot machines, only quarters and nickels.' I never saw another dime come out of that register again."

"That's brilliant!" Phil laughed.

"It was just good business. The slot machines showed an increase in revenue. I want to help my employers improve every aspect of their business. Not just in the kitchen, but all of it. But this isn't a casino, and we need to look at other revenue sources to fund growth so you can start closing on Saturdays," Mike glanced at Phil and raised his brows hopefully.

Phil returned his look with one of curiosity. "What's this closing on Saturday all about? This is not the first time you've mentioned that."

"Saturday is the Sabbath; the day the Lord has set aside for rest. It's the Fourth Commandment," Mike stated.

"Well, that would be impossible. It's our busiest day of the week. Are you like, real religious? What church do you belong to, anyway?" Phil asked.

"I'm a Christian, not any specific denomination. I am just a Christian, doing what the Bible says."

"Well, we were raised Catholic, and then joined a Baptist Church, but now we really only go to church a couple times a year."

"That's a start," Mike said, with an upbeat smile and his head nodding up and down like a dashboard bobble head.

"Are you always this positive?" Phil asked.

"I try to be," Mike replied, adding, "We're back."

As they approached the parking lot, it was obvious that

there were more cars than usual. Phil stopped in his tracks and looked at Mike, panic rising in his throat as he asked, "What do I do?"

"About what?" Mike responded calmly.

"Look Mike, I run the show here; I have for years. And then you come in with all your talent and I feel like I'm getting pushed out. It's like I'm suddenly a third wheel. Lord knows I need you, but I'm really feeling out of place in my own restaurant and I don't know what to do."

"You just learned your first lesson about pride. And came through it with flying colors."

"Pride?"

"Yes, pride. It has to be gone in order for God to truly work through you. And here in your kitchen, you are learning to let go of your pride so that others can shine brighter. Be humble, yet confident, and remember, it's God's kitchen. He has just authorized you to use it to glorify Him."

"Why am I so nervous?" Phil asked.

"Change is hard, especially when it is change that you didn't ask for. This is your first day on the job in a new dynamic, where you are no longer doing the heavy lifting. God has promoted you to a greater position, and that's why He sent me here to help you."

"God sent you here?" Phil asked.

"Yes He did," Mike replied with conviction.

"How can that be?" Phil wondered.

"With God, all things are possible. You're being offered more than just a promotion in your own business; you're being offered a job working for The Master Chef."

"I had a vision in the hospital about The Master Chef and I thought that was you. I even saw you and told my wife what you looked like."

"No, I'm not The Master Chef, Phil. The Master Chef is God, the Master of all the universe. When I say the Master Chef, I mean Him. Funny that He would send you a vision like that."

"So this vision I had was real? And you are sent by God?"

"Yes, I am. Don't think of it as such a stretch, Phil. God works through people to reach other people all the time. He spared your life to give you this opportunity to work for His kingdom, not just your earthly kitchen. And as far as this kitchen goes, we need to update your wardrobe. Come with me."

The two of them entered the restaurant through the back door, finding the activity level escalated several degrees from when they left.

"Getting a little busy back here!" Eddie shouted from behind the line.

"I'll be right there!" Mike replied.

In the office, Mike opened the closet door and pulled out a beautiful, brand new chef's coat in rich burgundy with black trim and black buttons, embroidered with 'Chef Phil' on the left chest. A black apron was stitched with green wording 'Eat Fresh'.

"Phil, I need you to wear this and host out front today. We have a good team in place, but we need your presence. Be social; conversation is the key to growth. Shake hands, kiss babies, and tell a few jokes."

"I can do that." Phil said, still admiring his new clothes.

"Good. Now listen. It's all about the flow at the front of the house. Rotate between servers, don't slam anybody." Mike was rushing the instructions, knowing that he needed to get on the main line. "And whatever you do, don't --"

"Mike! They need you!" Lisa interrupted.

"I'm there. How are you all up front?" Mike asked.

"Oh we're fine, four servers and a busboy. We've got this." Lisa replied.

"As Mike hurried out of the room, Phil followed asking, "Don't what? Don't what?" but it was too late to get a reply.

Mike went on the front line where there were twelve tickets hanging. He looked at the boys and said with a laugh, "Twelve tickets? That's it? I thought you were busy!"

Phil watched for a moment from the servers' station as Mike was recalling the orders and commanding the drops and pick-ups. His hands were as fast as lightning with impressive, precise accuracy. He even had time to high five his apprentices between two orders coming in to the window. Phil looked at Lisa in disbelief.

"I know," Lisa whispered. "He isn't even rushed right now."

Mike was moving like the wind. Grabbing a spatula, he

began flipping pancakes onto a plate, each one doing a full 360 before landing perfectly on the plate, which was then gracefully placed in the window for service.

"Amazing... Simply amazing," was all Phil could say.

For the next couple hours, the restaurant was bustling, but not too busy for them to handle. Around 11:00am it slowed down a bit, so Mike sent Eddie and Eric on a break and handled the line by himself. Phil came back to help, but Mike stopped him at the entryway. "Not in that outfit, you don't."

Phil took off his new coat and apron and began wiping down counters and looking at the few tickets that were left to serve.

"That was a lot of tables." Phil said.

"We turned well over three-hundred covers," Mike said.

"That's more than we normally serve on our busiest day," Phil added.

"Yeah, and it's only Tuesday," Mike replied.

Just then, Steve came in the door. Phil grabbed him in a big bear hug.

"How's my number one? I've missed you!" Phil and Steve had always had a special bond, but it was quite a statement for Phil to be so demonstrative, especially right in front of Mike.

"Doing good; I've missed you too!" Steve replied enthusiastically.

"You're not getting frustrated with all the changes going

on, are you?" Phil asked.

"No, not at all. Looks like we're going to need a little more help around here at night though."

"Every shift," Mike added.

"I think you're going to have to position yourself as more of a leader around here," Phil told Steve.

Noting Mike's nod of agreement, Steve commented, "I'm ready."

"How many covers did you turn?" Steve asked.

"I'm guessing about 325 for breakfast."

"You've got to be kidding me!" Steve exclaimed.

"Nope," Phil said.

"Wait till the new menus come out," Mike added. "What do people eat around here, anyway? I could really use some menu ideas, Steve. We need profit and productivity more than anything, but the menu needs to be fresh and reflect local tastes at the same time."

"I'll think about it and get some stuff written down," Steve said.

"Great!"

"Are you ready for a break?" Steve asked.

"Oh yeah," Mike replied. "That was almost four hours straight up here."

"Okay. I'll take over here, if you get the guys to stock the line and bring up the lunch specials."

"Works for me," Mike agreed, twirling his 8-inch chefs' knife and catching the handle.

As Mike made his exit from the front line, he checked in with Eric and Eddie to make sure they were getting the lunch service ready. Things were running smooth, and there was a sense of joy throughout the restaurant.

Jenny came in to help for lunch and was chatting with the kitchen team when Phil heard her voice.

"Jenny, Mike, come on in the office," Phil called.

'Yes dear," Jenny said, wiping sweat off her husband's brow with concern. "Are you okay?"

"Oh, I'm fine. Had one heck of a workout. I just looked at the computer; we had 360 covers for breakfast."

"Wow, did you really?"

"Yeah," Phil said, before taking a long drink of water and dropping down into his chair. "We're going to have to get a little more help in here. I'm just not physically ready to run around the restaurant like this yet."

"I propose that you close on Saturdays and divert the labor to the other shifts," Mike suggested.

"How did I know you were going to say that?" Phil said with a chuckle.

"What? Close on Saturday? That's the busiest day of the week!" Jenny protested.

"It used to be," Mike responded. "Right now, Monday through Friday is actually busier."

"We *are* generating enough cash flow on weekdays to justify closing on Saturdays." Phil said.

"Oh my, I didn't expect to hear that from you, Phil," Jenny said.

"Neither did I," added Mike, hoping his wish was about to be granted.

"Right now, this increase is only covering the additional labor that you've hired to take your place Phil," Jenny said. "Just do the numbers and you will see that there is no additional net profit. God has blessed in a mighty way to sustain us while you're recovering."

"She's right, you know," Mike confirmed.

"But if your mornings are going to be this strong, we will definitely need more help," Phil said. "What do we do here?"

"Hire more help, market the restaurant, and listen to God," Mike replied with a confident nod.

"I agree," Jenny said.

"Dr. Foster said they're starting construction on the new hospital and medical center, just a mile down the road," Mike commented. "That means more hungry customers, Phil."

"Along with other population increase and community growth coming this way too," Jenny added.

"Can we get together tonight, just the three of us? We need to do a little homework and pray about this," Phil suggested.

"Sure. God is calling you for a number of reasons, Phil." Mike challenged him. "This second chance at health, that's not really what God is preparing you for. He is preparing you for a second chance at *life*. I know you are both Christians, but are you willing to dedicate your lives to living the way Christ is asking you to live? We close at 7pm; does that time work for you two to meet up?" Phil and Jenny nodded in agreement as Mike continued, "I need to pray too. Lunch is set, and I have to go. I'll see you tonight."

As he left the room Jenny glanced at Phil and raised her brow. "He is quite the spiritually connected person," she said.

"Yes, he is. And God sent him to us," Phil said.

"Well, there's no doubt about that."

"No, Jenny; God *really* sent him to us."

"What? How do you mean?" Jenny asked, her expression quizzical.

"Remember that day in the hospital when I told you what Mike looked like before you ever told me about him?" Phil asked.

"Now that you mention it, yes I do," Jenny said, recalling the day.

"I had a vision of him clear as day, and I knew that God had sent him. Then this morning when we were taking a walk after breakfast, he told me that God did indeed send him to us."

"Well, it could just be a coincidence," Jenny suggested.

"No, sweetheart. God literally told Mike to come here for a purpose, and He literally told me that He was sending me a helper."

"I think that's great. With God, all things are possible," Jenny said.

"That's exactly what Mike said this morning!" Phil exclaimed.

"Well, it's true," Jenny agreed.

Phil gazed at his wife intently. "Mike wants us to close on Saturdays."

"Yes, I know, and I'm not against looking into that, but where are you going with this? Are we just supposed to let him run the whole show? Don't forget, you are still the boss," Jenny reminded him firmly.

Now that he was convicted, Phil couldn't squelch desire in his heart to do the right thing; it was just a matter of getting Jenny on board with him. He took her hands in his and said, "When God sends you wise counsel, you listen. We may not always understand the decisions He calls us to make, but I pray that we make the right ones."

Jenny nodded. "I think we need to take Mike's lead and let's just pray about this today. Look, I've got lunch covered, why don't you go home and get some rest, and I'll see you tonight."

"I will, but first I want to run down to the City Planner's office and find out about the new development plans around here."

"Okay. Love you." Jenny kissed Phil on her way out the

door.

"Love you too."

After a quick stop at the City Planner's office, Phil went home for that well-deserved rest.

Shaken

…. >> … Phil awoke with a jolt and realized that he had been dreaming about the past, when Mike was growing their business. Suddenly the bed was shaking, but it wasn't Jenny trying to rouse him. Phil looked frantically around the room. Seeing the walls shaking, he jumped to his feet as panic set in. There was no doubt that this was an earthquake.

"Jenny?" Phil shouted, "Are you here?"

"Yes, I'm right here!" Jenny yelled back above the roar. It sounded as if a locomotive was thundering through the house, and would soon look like it, too.

"We've got to get out of here!" Phil grabbed Jenny's hand and they raced out of the house, dodging falling objects as the ceiling began to collapse. The walls were crumbling around them as though the house was made of toothpicks. The earth continued to shake as they embraced on the front lawn, their eyes constantly scanning to make sure they weren't in the path of any falling trees and debris. A few minutes seemed like hours in the anxiety of the moment.

This was no ordinary earthquake, especially for this Midwest town where there had never been a quake of any magnitude. Pockets of flames and smoke filled the sky across the horizon. It wouldn't take a press conference to tell that the damage was severe.

Without warning, a tree toppled over onto the garage, barely sparing the truck in the driveway. Just as the earth calmed enough to allow Phil and Jenny to stand to their feet, another quake brought them once again to their knees. The tremors continued for what seemed like hours. Every time they would attempt to go inside to assess the damage, the shaking would resume with gusto.

Phil and Jenny walked to the end of the driveway, looking up and down the road. The scattered trees and downed power lines made it obvious that traveling anywhere was most likely out of the question.

"What is going on Phil?" Jenny asked. "Is the world coming to an end?"

"I don't think so, but Mike did say there would be earthquakes in diverse places."

"I was just dreaming about those days," Jenny said.

"Really? Me too!" Phil exclaimed.

"Do you remember that meeting we had with Mike about closing on the Sabbath?" Jenny asked.

"Like it was yesterday," Phil said. "My, how long ago was that... Fifteen years?"

"Pretty close. Is this a sign for us to go into the wilderness?" Jenny asked.

"I'm really not sure, we need to go to the Lord in prayer."

"Yes we do, Phil. Please, please." Jenny replied anxiously, as they drew close together and bowed their heads.

"Oh Heavenly Father, to Whom we have dedicated our lives, we come to You with thanks. Thank You for sparing us at this time. Although we would rather be caught up in the clouds with You at this very moment, we know You have Your reasons and ways. Please Lord, forgive us of our sins, purify our hearts and minds with a power that can only come from You." Phil continued as the ground began to tremble once more. "Lord, You are the giver and taker of life, and we thank You for Your protecting love. We need You Father, for the discernment that will direct our path. We are in the palm of Your hand, with a peace and calm that cannot be shaken. Not by an earthquake, and not by Satan's attempts to cause us to fear and worry. We are always on the solid rock of Your mercy and grace. Be with us Lord. In Jesus' name we pray, Amen."

Jenny and Phil continued in prayer for well over an hour. A sense of calm and deep peace stirred their hearts as they heard the voice of God saying, 'Remember the lessons The Master Chef has taught you. Time is shorter than you think. Be still until you are called to move. Be still.'

Jenny looked up at Phil with tears in her eyes, knowing they had truly heard the voice of God. Even though Phil had heard God speak to him before, Jenny always had her doubts. Shame and regret washed over her now, but looking into Phil's eyes, as she was met with his understanding gaze, she knew no apology was necessary.

"Be Still," Phil said gently.

"Well, we had better get situated," Jenny said. "It's going to be chilly tonight."

The early summer weather was a blessing in a situation without electricity, and Phil had a large generator with plenty of fuel, but they needed to figure out where to take shelter for the night.

Although the front of the house was totally collapsed with one story upon another, the kitchen and back covered patio seemed to be solid. Phil managed to retrieve blankets and pillows out of a couple of rooms, and began to look for access to a mattress. Crawling into the garage, he realized he was able to stand upright inside the garage. Every area that had two stories was history, but the single-story structures were still stable.

"Be careful Phil!" Jenny shouted with concern.

Moments later, Jenny heard the firing up of the chainsaw. The sound guided her to the far side of the house, where she saw the blade coming through a partially crushed door. In no time at all, Phil came walking through the side door of the garage, his chest puffed and a proud grin on his face.

When Jenny saw him, she couldn't help but laugh, and Phil couldn't help but join her.

"The garage is very accessible from here."

"Hey!" Jenny shouted. "We have the trailer!"

A proverbial light bulb went off in both their minds, directing them to the backside of their steel pole barn. On the far side was their 30-foot trailer nestled in its custom built port. It was completely unharmed - a gift of protection from the hand of God.

"And you didn't want me to buy this," Phil chuckled, thoroughly enjoying his newfound vindication from the guilt of arguments past.

"Well, now we have a place to stay with plenty of fuel, plenty of water in the rain catchers and plenty of food, too. God has provided for all of our needs, so I guess you're forgiven," Jenny said, grinning.

As they went about gathering up items and clearing out

access ways as much as possible, it was evident that the darkness would soon overtake them and force the end of their work for the day. Phil was able to fire up the truck and move it back behind the barn next to the trailer and out of visibility from the road. As the skies darkened, the glow of numerous fires became more prevalent, especially toward town.

What could be going on? How bad was it for others? And how much worse could it get? They laid on their bed in the silence of the night, holding each other. Few words were spoken as they both flashed-back to those days when the Master Chef was teaching them through Mike. Trying to remember every word that Mike said to them over the years was difficult, but the day of the meeting stood out more than any other.

The Decision

.... <<... Phil awoke from his nap and headed down to the restaurant for the evening meeting. As he entered the open but empty restaurant, Jenny was setting up a table for them to have dinner. The smell of meatloaf with mashed potatoes and gravy were a delight to the senses, especially as they were not on the menu.

Jenny glanced up and smiled. "You're 10 minutes early."

"And showered, too." Phil replied.

Mike emerged from the kitchen with a big salad and placed it at the table. He put his arm around Phil and walked him to the front door. Locking the door and turning out the lights, Mike whispered to Phil, "Do you remember how jealous Satan was when Jesus was having private meetings with God?" Mike motioned to the kitchen where Steve was finishing up.

"Yes, I do." Phil replied. He then walked over to the kitchen and called Steve, "Come on Steve, we need you with us."

Once they were all seated and ready to eat, Mike prayed, "Lord, we are here to serve You in every way possible, and with these meetings, we pray for Your power and glory to be poured out upon us. Be with us and help us to make good decisions and continue to glorify Your name in everything we do. May Thy will be done. And bless this food which comes from Your hands, to nourish our bodies for Your service. Amen."

"Amen," The others echoed.

"Now that's the best idea I have heard in years, praying before a meeting starts," Jenny said.

"I like it too," Steve added. "It's like it takes a big burden off the whole meeting."

"Amen to that," Phil agreed.

"The salad is for Phil, and we get the meatloaf," Jenny said. "Doctor's orders."

"Ohhhh, that's just wrong!" Phil pouted.

Mike took a huge slab of mouthwatering meatloaf and placed it on Phil's plate, then added the mashed potatoes and smothered it all with gravy.

"You did such a good job today, here is your reward," Mike said with a smile. "And tomorrow, we're walking an extra mile."

Everyone watched as Phil prepared to take a bite, then hesitated, a mixture of frustration and guilt on his face. Sighing, he dropped the fork and pushed his plate away. "Give me my stupid salad," he muttered. Everyone applauded, cheering his ability to resist temptation.

"Seriously now Captain," Mike said. "I need you to at least take a bite, because I want to put this item on the dinner menu."

Phil took a small bite and smiled with approval. "It's good. It's *really* good." Savoring another little bite, he said, "You just can't get any better than that!"

"Well, it does get better," Mike said, grinning.

Everyone looked at him with curiosity.

"It's vegan! All plant-based. No animal products whatsoever!" Mike exclaimed.

"It's vegan?" Phil asked incredulously.

"Yep. You can eat the whole thing. No beef, no cholesterol, no fat. Pretty cool, huh?"

"You have got to be kidding me," Steve said.

"This tastes great!" Jenny added.

"And the sweet part is that we can sell this for an extra couple bucks, because it's healthy; yet the food cost is actually half the price of a regular meatloaf."

"I'm sold!" Phil said, still shocked that something this delicious could be so healthy.

"Me too," Steve said. "Is it easy to make?"

"Oh yeah, we can batch them and freeze them too. I also have a vegan lasagna that tastes better than any cheese lasagna you will ever find. You want vegan ice cream?" Mike asked. Seeing the enthusiastic nods from the others, whose mouths were filled with the amazing "meat" loaf, he continued. "I think what we can do is transform a lot of this menu into a healthy menu, giving you a niche that the competition won't be able to move in on."

"I really like that too." Phil said.

"And you could end up being the poster child for it. You were pushing 400 pounds, and we will get all the excess weight off of you."

"Hey!" Steve interrupted. "We could have the slogan 'Never trust a fat chef!' instead of 'Never trust a skinny chef.'" Everyone laughed until they had tears in their eyes.

As the conversation continued with everyone brainstorming together, it was a real pleasure for all of them to socialize in such a collaborative way. Some ideas were bit too extreme to be considered reasonable possibilities, while others had real potential.

After a while, Mike shifted the conversation to a more serious tone. "With all these great ideas, I think we could still close for the Sabbath."

"What's with this Sabbath?" Steve asked. "Do you want us to close on Sundays?"

"Actually, Mike here thinks we should close on Saturdays," Phil said.

"Well, I don't see that. That's one of the busiest days of the week," Steve said.

"Today was busier than any day of the week you've ever had," Mike replied.

"Is this a Biblical truth?" Jenny asked.

"It's the fourth commandment," Steve said.

Phil looked at Steve in surprise. "You know that?"

"Sure I do. I went to Sunday school," Steve chuckled. "But I thought the Sabbath was Sunday, not Saturday."

"No, the Sabbath is from sunset Friday to sunset Saturday," Mike explained. "Both the old and new testaments confirm that the Sabbath is Saturday. It always has been and always will be. It was man that attempted to change the Sabbath. Well, actually, it was Satan's deception more than man's. Man was just the unknowing pawn in Satan's plan to keep people from obeying God's commandments." Mike pulled out his Bible to start searching scriptures.

"Well let's look at this for a minute," Jenny said. "Hobby Lobby closes on Sunday. Chik-Fil A closes on Sunday too - even in the mall. Let's just look at this possibility for a minute."

"That's Sunday; I want to know about this Saturday thing," Steve said. "I mean, I was thrilled to have Mike working Sundays so I could have them off, but how do you know Saturday is the Sabbath when everyone observes Sunday?"

"Let me explain," Mike began. "You all know that 30 million Jews still honor the Sabbath on Saturday, and that they have been doing that throughout all of their days, right?" As the others nodded in agreement, he continued. "And you know that all the apostles in the New Testament kept the Sabbath, right? Can any of you show me anywhere in the Bible where Jesus changed the Sabbath from Saturday, the seventh day, to Sunday the first day? Anyone? No? That's because it's not there! Nowhere in the Bible was the Sabbath ever changed. Ever."
"So why do Christians honor Sunday as the Sabbath?" Steve asked.

"Well, it wasn't until hundreds of years after the Bible was written, when Constantine the Emperor of Rome declared Sunday a day of rest in order to draw the Pagans into the church. Sunday was the day on which the pagans worshiped their sun gods, and Constantine knew it would be easier to convert them to Christianity if he kept their festival day. For a while, both days were kept, but the Sabbath was traditionally kept as a day of fasting, while Sunday was a day of feasting, so the new converts to Christianity enjoyed the Sunday celebration but considered the Sabbath a burden.

"Also, the Sabbath was associated with the Jews, from whom the Christians wanted to distance themselves. Eventually, the pagan Sunday became more and more prevalent as a day of worship. But even then, many Christians still honored the true Sabbath from sunset Friday to sunset Saturday. Satan brought the transformation about so slowly and cleverly that no one really questioned it. It took another couple hundred years for the Sabbath to be almost completely wiped out and regarded solely as an expression of the Jewish faith. But that wasn't enough for Satan. He has such hatred for God's law that he wasn't satisfied until he had persuaded church authorities to make Sunday observance a requirement, with punishment for anyone who insisted on hanging on to the seventh-day Sabbath. In the Dark Ages, the church would kill any Christians that were not honoring Sunday."

"Well, that all makes so much sense," Jenny said.

"It sure does," Phil added.

"You see friends, we are now living in a generation that really doesn't know any better, because they don't know their Bibles. They may know a few key scriptures, but most people haven't truly studied God's word or developed a personal relationship with Christ. They are living in deception, thereby continually breaking God's commandments."

"Yeah, just look at this world today; it is an absolute mess." Steve said.

"And if we are a Christian nation, why are most businesses

open on Sunday?" Jenny asked.

"Good point," Mike said.

"If the Christian world actually believed what the Bible says, then why are they all open on what they *think* is the Sabbath?" Steve asked.

"It's certainly not godly for someone who claims to be a Christian, not knowing the truth about Saturday being the Sabbath, to not honor Sunday," Mike explained. "Satan's agenda is to get everyone to break God's commandments, even in ignorance. He will trick and deceive you. Whatever it takes."

"Look at the reality of it. Right now, you break God's commandments. Whether you believe the Sabbath is Sunday or Saturday or Wednesday, you are certainly breaking God's commandments because you are open seven days a week."

"He's right you know," Phil said.

"So are you going to close on the Sabbath and honor God, or are you going to continue to work seven days a week and disobey God?" Mike asked.

"We have a serious decision to make here," Jenny said, looking at Phil.

"I would like to just say one thing here, and that is that God has given me a second chance at life and I want to do whatever He asks of me. But closing on Saturdays seems like financial suicide. I have people relying on this business," Phil said, gesturing toward Steve. "We've got to know this will work. What would happen if the general Christian population starts boycotting us for going against the grain of their misinformed tradition?"

"They will, Phil," Mike said. "That's in the Bible too."

Phil shook his head in frustration. "This is way too big of a risk to take! Can you assure me that we can produce enough profit to provide for everyone's needs?"

Mike thought for a moment and said, "Lisa made over one hundred dollars in tips today. With that kind of shift, she can easily work one less day a week."

"Speaking of Lisa," Jenny giggled, "I think she and Steve would make a cute couple!"

"I don't think so!" Steve said, blushing furiously. "I'm not really into red heads."

"Oh, baloney!" Phil teased, "You like *every* woman, don't you, tiger?"

Steve laughed and shook his head. "What I *really* like is my single life, so let's just get on with this meeting."

"Phil," Mike said in a serious tone, "there are no guarantees in life. God does not say, 'I will prove Myself, then you will believe.' He says, 'Trust and obey, and *then* I will prove Myself to you.'

"I have a scripture for you," Mike continued. "This is from Isaiah 58: 'If you turn away your foot from doing your own pleasure on My holy Sabbath day, And call the Sabbath a delight and the holy *day* of the Lord honorable, and shall honor Him, not doing your own ways, nor finding your own pleasure, nor speaking *your own* words, then you shall delight yourself in the Lord; And I will cause you to ride on the high places of the earth, And feed you with the heritage of Jacob your father. The mouth of the Lord has spoken.'"

Everyone sat in thoughtful silence.

"You see, it's IF and THEN. IF you will obey, THEN God can bless you in an amazing way. I can't guarantee I'll be here forever, but I promise I will see you through this. Steve has talent, and God will increase it. You are all being offered a job right now – you're being called to work for The Master Chef. If you will trust Him, He will do things for this business and you personally that you can't even imagine. Now, it's getting late, and I have the AM shift, and Phil has a walking class in the morning. Here is a paper about the Sabbath, with all the undisputed evidence, scriptures, and everything you need to research it for yourselves. Just the most cursory study is enough to convince anyone of the truth of the Sabbath. Now each of you must study, pray and decide for yourselves. I'll see you all tomorrow."

"You guys go ahead, I'll get all this," Steve said, gesturing toward the messy table. "And as far as my vote goes, I'll do whatever you want me to do boss, but I'm great with the Saturday/Sabbath closing."

As the others left, Steve cleaned up. When he was finished, he knelt alone in the silence and prayed.

That night at home, Phil and Jenny took a better look at the sheet Mike had created about the Sabbath. It was quite a surprise to them how many scriptures that were included on the sheet.

"Look at this Phil," Jenny said. "We know about the fourth commandment in Exodus 20:8 like Mike explained, but this second point is quite interesting. It says that Exodus 31:16 calls the Sabbath a 'perpetual covenant,' meaning forever and ever, never to be changed."

"You know Jenny, I've talked to Mike all about this before and there really is no disputing that Saturday is the Sabbath," Phil said.

Jenny nodded and read some more. "In fact, this says that the Hebrew translation for 'perpetual' is actually defined as 'without end, ages or endless time, eternal, and everlasting'. Mike sure did his homework."

"He really did. And the question is; are we going to follow our conviction and do the right thing? Will we trust God and be obedient to His word, or do we turn our backs on what we know to be true?"

"He's got scriptures here showing that Jesus kept the Sabbath too. Luke 4:16 and Mathew 5:17... And all the scriptures showing how attempts would be made to change God's law. In Daniel 7:25 it says that 'they will intend to change times and laws. Phil, there is so much we don't know!"

"Yes there is, but the problem here is with what we do know. And the question is still present: aren't we responsible to adhere to the knowledge we have?"

"I believe we are, but I think we need to sleep on it and maybe we'll have a better perspective in the morning," Jenny concluded.

The next morning Phil awoke early and, for the first time in his life, his knees hit the ground before his feet. After he had been praying for some time, Jenny awoke and saw him kneeling by the bed. As he looked up and their eyes met, Jenny knew what his answer was. She nodded in agreement and went back to sleep.

When Phil arrived at the restaurant, Mike already had his breakfast ready and sitting in the warmer.

"Today's special, whole wheat cinnamon swirl pancakes," Mike said. "I can't leave for our walk until I get the lunch specials done. We just had an early rush of construction workers, so give me 30 minutes and I'll be ready."

"Great, I'll go check yesterday's totals," Phil said, heading toward his office.

Mike called Sally, Terry and Beth into the kitchen to check in and make sure everything was going well. Lisa was on the later shift, so the three of them were going to have to handle things without her today.

"We're going to have to do things a little different today, ladies," Mike said. "I need to be expediting from the servers' line and you three are going to have to handle the front with Phil. Don't worry about dropping toast or getting beverages, I'll take care of all that. Just get the orders into the computer and get to the next table. I'm going to take a walk with Phil, and then be back before the breakfast rush. If it's hitting early, call me."

"I think we'll totally rock this," Sally said.

People had given her the nickname Valley Sally because of the valley girl vernacular she'd picked up growing up in Southern California. Even though she looked and talked like a bubble-headed bleach blond, she was a smart girl and could definitely hustle. Beth, on the other hand was like a bull in a china shop, and had the large frame to go with it. Everyone who met her gravitated toward her jolly smile and heart of gold. But when it came to work, she moved like a tornado, sometimes running people down in her haste. Terry was the shy one. With her simple, unadorned appearance and plain farm girl sweetness, she fit right in with the country atmosphere. Having these three on any shift was certainly a study in opposites.

"Yeah, we can do this," Beth said.

After putting a couple pans of food in the oven, Mike began filling other pans with vegetables and rice. With the shortage in help, lunch had to be ready early today.

Eddie and Eric were in the kitchen, ready to go.

"Well Chef, are we going to be as busy as we were yesterday?" Eddie asked.

"Probably, but you two will have to handle it on your own today," Mike replied.

"What?" Eric's head snapped up in surprise and concern.

"Don't worry, I'll be right on the other side of the window. Just remember the fundamentals: keep the hash brown station full, drop those meats as soon as the order comes in, and keep the cakes grill busy so you don't get backed up on it. And here's a new trick for you."

Mike lined up ten plates, topping each one with kale and an orange twist. Then he stacked another level of plates, balancing them on top of the edges of the other plates and then did a third and fourth row.

"That's so cool!" Eddie exclaimed, examining the pyramid of pre-garnished plates.

"If you keep up on these, you'll really zoom," Mike replied.

Phil came in and saw the pyramid, now five levels high. "Don't you guys got nothing better to do?" He laughed.

"Just getting them ready for the rush, Captain. You ready to go?" Mike asked.

"Yes, and we're going east today. I want to show you something."

"Okay, let's go. We'll see you guys in less than an hour," Mike called back to Sally and the brothers.

It was a brisk cold morning, with the grey skies predicting their last snow of the year, but that was always great walking weather. As they started out, Mike kept silent, wondering what Phil had on his mind.

"Well, Mike," Phil said with a look of deep concern, "I want to show you what's going on over here beyond this hill. I went to the city yesterday and discovered a couple of key issues that we need to consider before making any big decisions."

"Okay," Mike said, listening closely.

"See here, it's mostly scattered houses with everybody having a dozen or so acres, and with so many different owners, it's really difficult to get enough people together to develop it, and that will make development quite slow around the restaurant. But right over this hill, there are thousands of acres being developed."

As they walked to the top of the hill, they looked out at a seemingly endless valley of barren fields and dirt roads.

"That's where the new hospital is going," Phil said, pointing toward the dust rising from a couple of earthmovers. "They're building a four-hundred room hospital and full medical center."

"This is only about a mile from the restaurant, right?" Mike asked.

"1.4 miles, to be exact," Phil replied.
"Is this going to be a master planned community, with shops, more restaurants, and food store?" Mike asked.

"Yes, and houses, apartments, and a higher population," Phil added.

So this is good, and this is bad," Mike said.

"More competition and more places to eat are bad, but more people and more dollars in the community is good," Phil mused. "The sweet part about this is that the money and the people generally come in before the commerce business arrives, so we can focus on building our reputation before the competition arrives."

As they walked back, Mike asked, "Is this road going to be the main road into town?"

"Well, no, but it is the best shortcut to every home on the north side of town. Plus it's all four and five lane roads on the city's map," Phil responded.

"Which means lots of construction," Mike said.

"Yes, but only to the right, there where the traffic light is going to go. Where my property is, we already have five lanes, so we won't get the construction blocking our access."

Mike thought for a minute. "That's good. We do have a couple of challenges, and mostly targets of demographics to capitalize on."

Phil agreed. "Construction workers will be our primary target, while building up our reputation in the community. Then, as the construction wave gradually reduces, we'll increase the local draw."

"Makes sense, and I think we can do this," Mike said confidently.

"We need to go for it all," Phil said, his excitement growing. "And when I say go for it all, I mean we need to take advantage of every dollar we can get. We need the new menus, we need the new hours, and we need to take the banquet room and convert it into dining.

"And... We want to close on the Sabbath," Phil said, his face beaming. He reached out and drew a delighted Mike in for a bear hug. "We're not doing this *for* you, we're doing this *because* of you. The Sabbath is such a no-brainer for us, we can't help but want to do this. We love the Lord, and we want to serve the Lord to the best of our abilities. And we want you to help orchestrate everything that needs to be done to establish this restaurant that He has given us as a shining light in the community. Will you help us do this for Him?"

"That's why He sent me here," Mike said, smiling.

"Well, let's head back and get through the lunch rush, and then I want you to hire whomever you need to build up the business. Let's keep focused on the bigger picture."

"You've got it, Captain," Mike said. "I'll have everything drawn up by the first of next week."

"We'll have to start by having a meeting with all of the employees. Do you think Friday evening will work for everyone?" Phil asked.

"Yes, let's close at 5:00pm on Friday, and head straight into the meeting from there," Mike said.

Phil nodded. "Perfect."

Amen!

On Friday, the entire team gathered together and Mike and Phil got right down to business.

"Hello everyone," Mike began. "I would like to start by making sure everyone's acquainted with everybody else. You'd never know we had this many people working here until we all come together. Just to let you know, we need to hire some additional staff over the next few weeks - four more cooks, three more dishwashers and two more servers for sure. If you know anyone who would be a good fit here, please let them know and send them our way."

Phil took over from there, getting right to the point. "Thank you all for coming out for this meeting. As you probably know, we have been getting much busier around here and we are anticipating that it is going to get busier still, so we are going to have a series of meetings to gear up for this increased volume. These meetings are for the purposes of brainstorming ideas as a group, and to keep everyone updated and abreast of any changes."

"The first thing I want you all to understand is that we are running this business as a gift from God. For His purposes and His glory. Just like Hobby Lobby, Chick-fil-A, and hundreds of other successful businesses around the world, we want to honoring God in all that we do. On that note, let's open with prayer. Steve, will you offer prayer for us?"

"Sure... Lord in heaven, we come before You this day to praise and worship Your holy name. We thank You for the blessings that You have poured down upon us. Be with us today, putting our own intentions aside, to be filled with Your desires, so that Your will may be done. In Jesus' name, Amen."

"Amen." Everyone echoed.

"Wait a minute, did you hear that?" Mike asked.

"Hear what?" Lisa asked.

"Everyone say Amen again."

"Amen."

"Louder!"

"Amen!"

"Shout it!" Mike hollered.

"AMEN!"

"Wow!" Mike said. "I think we could be that 'Amen' restaurant."

"Oh, yes! Wouldn't it be cool if we found ways to say 'Amen' and did it whenever we could?" Jenny's face lit up in excitement.

"Amen?" Joy asked hesitantly.

"Exactly," Mike said, smiling at Joy, whose name truly suited her, for she really was a joy to be around. She was the tallest of the bunch, and probably the best team player of all. There really was nothing she wouldn't do for anyone.

"Well, Amen!" Phil said. "We're going to make some serious changes these next few weeks, and then once we've adjusted to the new menus and other changes, we'll have a marketing blitz to get the word out."

"Amen." Kimmie giggled, and was promptly rewarded with a thumbs up from Mike.

"First things first," Phil added." How have things been going for the last couple months while I've been recovering?"

"Great," "Fantastic," "Everything's been terrific," the group replied, nodding and looking at one another in confirmation.

"Wonderful," Phil smiled. I believe that is largely due to Mike and the wonderful talents God has given him."

"Amen!" Steve shouted, eliciting applause from the rest of the group.

"We also have some major construction that is going on about a mile away. There will be literally thousands of people coming in and out of this area for the next couple of years with a new hospital and over a dozen other developments surrounding it," Phil continued. "Who have we been serving lately?"

"Sally spoke up. "It's totally the super cute construction workers in the morning."

"And a lot of suits throughout the day," Lisa added.

"But not on the weekends, right?" Phil asked.

"No, the weekends have totally been slower than the weekdays. It's a total bummer, you know?" Sally said.

"Which isn't normal, is it?" Phil asked.

"Totally not." Sally replied, rolling her eyes dramatically.

"Well, we are changing our business plan as well," Phil continued. "As of today, we are going to be closed on the weekends."

A uniform gasp rose from the shocked employees, then everyone began to talk at once, their questions pelting Phil like bullets from a BB gun.

"What?" "Are you serious?" "Why?" "How can we do that?"

Phil held up his hand to silence the group. "From now on, we're going to focus our efforts on the Monday through Friday business crowd.

"But I make like big bucks on the weekends. I totally can't afford to lose a day," Sally said, panic in her voice.

"I'll give you my shift, if you need it," Joy offered kindly.

"Nobody is going to lose a day," Jenny interjected. You'll all have plenty of shifts on the weekdays, when we are so desperately in need of more staff.

"Lisa, how much were your tips today?" Phil asked.

"$140.00." Lisa replied.

"WHAT?" Kimmie shrieked. "Are you serious?"

"Is that good?" Mike asked.

"It's more than double what I used to do," Lisa replied.

"So you're making more in four days than you used to in

five?" Phil asked.

Lisa smiled, and said with a chuckling agreement, "Well, yeah, I guess I am."

"Hey girlfriend," Sally chimed in. "Like, nobody in town is pulling those kind of digits."

"And with the new menus producing a slightly higher ticket average, tips will go up too," Mike said. "We are going to open on Sundays in about four or six weeks from now, but it's going to be for a flat rate Sunday Buffet; the kind of buffet that blows people away. We'll have a line out the door of people waiting to get in."

"Amen!" a couple of voices responded.

Phil spoke again, sharing his heart with the group. "As you all know, I am a Christian who just got a second chance at life, and I just want to do God's will in everything I do. And since I have discovered that Saturday is the seventh-day Sabbath that the Bible repeatedly points to, I want to honor God by observing that day of rest the way He asks us to. Now, I'm not going to get into a full discussion about the Sabbath today. I know that Mike has talked to many of you about it, and here are two full pages all about the topic if you want to study it out for yourself. And I suggest you do. But everyone who works for me will always have off from sunset Friday to sunset Saturday for rest with family and worship the Lord if they choose to do so."

"AMEN!" Steve shouted, followed by a chorus of 'Amens' from the others.

"Mike is going to be orchestrating this whole transition. Steve will be the kitchen leader, and Lisa is going to be the AM front of house leader, with Sally leading the PM shift.

Are we all good with this?"

"Amen!" The group shouted in unison, startling Phil.

"This 'Amen' thing is going to be quite a sensation," he chuckled. "Well Mike, I'll turn the floor back over to you now. What do you have for us?"

"The first thing I want to do is ask a question. What do you all think we need?

Phil has lots of money to spend." Mike laughed and put his arm around Phil. "I love spending other people's money."

"Our bathrooms are disgusting," Lisa said.

"They're clean, just old looking," Jenny interjected.

"We need some fresh paint," Eddie pointed out.

"Inside and out," Terri added.

"And I'd love to have another busser station at the far side of the dining room, so we don't have to run so far during the rush hours," Beth pointed out.

"Yeah, we totally need one over there!" Sally agreed.

"I would really like to see some better uniforms," Terri added. I mean, polo shirts are fine, but if you're going to kick it up, kick it up." If there was one thing Terri had, it was an eye for perfection.

"We're going to need designated hosts, too, Kimmie said.

"Anything else?" Mike asked as Jenny wrote down the suggestions.

"If you really want to get carried away, expand the counter. People are always, always waiting for a seat," Terri commented.

"Well, you've given us some great ideas to work on. We'll start by getting a sign in the window that says we will be closed on the weekends for remodeling for the next six weeks," Mike said.

"That's a totally great idea," Sally said.

"And anyone who wants to come in on Sundays and volunteer some free time doing all these things is more than welcome," Phil said.
"FREE?" Phil's suggestion was met with a less than enthusiastic response from the group.

"It's either that, or I can take away the raise I just gave everybody."

"AMEN!" everyone shouted, laughing.

"Servers, you already got your raise in the increased tips, but the rest of the team, you've got another dollar an hour coming your way."

Brothers Eric and Eddie whooped and high-fived each other. "That's on top of the raise we just got for the kitchen promotion, right?" Eric asked.

"That's right. I want this team to be the highest paid team in town," Phil replied. So let's get this property looking and operating its best and let God do the rest. Amen?"

"AMEN!" the others shouted in unison.

"Now," Mike said, changing gears, "on the spiritual side, I have a few more things to say before I let you go. From talking to you all, I know that we are all Christians here." Mike paused for a moment, then continued. "But to what degree? We have all been placed into this upside-down world and really need God's discernment to filter through what is the truth and what are the lies. I want you all to know that I am not here to push religion on anybody, and neither should anyone else. Spreading the gospel is a privilege, and it's wonderful when God presents those opportunities. But God never wants us to force our views on someone who is resistant. That will just build up bigger walls of separation. People need to discover their own the path to the Lord.

"I'd like to share with you the simplicity of salvation. Since we all understand food, I'll use a recipe analogy. The simplicity of salvation is developed with a few key ingredients. As with any great recipe however, when one of the ingredients is missing, the end result is not the same. Churches today bombard us with messages of grace, faith and hope, promising salvation, but focusing heavily on only one or two of these ingredients. But is that really the 'recipe' for salvation? Can grace save us if there is no faith? Is there saving faith without obedience? Let's face it; we are all hungry for answers, and starving because the recipe we've been following comes from the kitchens of men, and is incomplete. But when we follow the recipe given to us by The Master Chef, we will finally have the finished product, and it tastes better than we could ever imagine.

"When I discovered The Master Chef's recipe for our salvation, I realized that it's so simple that anyone can make it, but so few have been willing to try it, or to share it with others. As a result, the recipe has become so rare that most people don't know it exists, and of those who do, many don't know where to find it. There are also a lot of counterfeit recipes out there, claiming to be the original, but they never turn out right. But once you find the recipe, if you're willing to share it, people will come to you to learn what The Master Chef has taught you. One of your primary goals as an apprentice is to mentor others in the art of cooking, in so they too can develop their own relationship with The Master Chef, and then share His recipe with others. He never turns anyone away."

"Wait a minute," Kimmie interjected. "Aren't you the Master Chef, or am I missing something here?"

"Yeah, I thought you were the Chef," Joy said. "Is it Phil then?"

Everyone laughed, waiting for Mike to sort out the confusion.

"No," Mike explained, "I'm not The Master Chef. There is only one Master Chef, The Master of the entire universe. He is the one who trained me, who gave me my talents and abilities. He has given each of us unique gifts to use and share. He has called me to share His recipe with you so that you can pass it on to others."

"So, The Master Chef is Christ?" Eric asked.

"That's right," Mike continued. "The Master Chef trains His team, then they branch out to culinary posts around the world to serve His truth and share the recipe. Everyone on The Master Chef's team is called to help. In fact, He is calling every single one of us into kitchens of outreach to finish the work so we can all go home. Paraphrasing Luke 10:2, it says, 'then the Master Chef said to them, the harvest truly *is* great, but the laborers *are too* few; therefore pray to the Lord of the harvest to send out laborers into His harvest.'

"See, The Master Chef is hiring! Just like we are hiring here in our earthly restaurant, He is looking for every single person He can find to fill His open positions. It doesn't matter what your qualifications are; He will accept you! He will provide you with the tools and talent you need to become an active and valuable part of His team. Don't be shy, The Master Chef has never turned anyone away. Never.

"You may not be too sure about The Master Chef right now, and that's OK. Even if you know nothing about His long list of credentials, or the wonderful way He cares for His team, look into this offer. I suggest researching any individual or company or you are considering working for, and The Master Chef is no exception. Do a little homework on His background and what He offers, and I guarantee you will find out that His record is without blemish. Ask any of His team members, and they will tell you that He is absolutely the best Leader they have ever worked for."

"Are you talking about yourself now, or God still?" Edith asked. "Because it sure sounds like you."

"That's what I thought too," Eric said.

"No, I'm still talking about God. Just to let you know up front, The Master Chef has never fired anyone, but I will," Mike said, smiling at Eddie as everyone laughed. "With God, there are many who walk away when they discover that it is not always easy to live up the Master Chef's standards, but He will always provide a way for those who are sincere. Rest assured, if you are willing, He is faithful and has more patience than we have ever experienced. And just to let you in on a little secret, His benefits package and retirement plan are absolutely phenomenal. I guess you could say that they're literally out of this world. You actually receive a full pension for eternity!"

"Yeah!" Eddie shouted, "You gotta love that!"

"That's right! An all-expenses paid retirement!" Edith rejoiced, "And I'm the oldest one here, so I'm the closest to retiring."

"You are guaranteed a home beyond your wildest imaginations, Edith. Sorry, but there is no health care, because with perfect health, you'll never be sick again. Vacation time will be thing of the past. Your future with The Master Chef will be absolute bliss.

"You would be an absolute fool to not take The Master Chef's offer. Sadly, so many turn Him away because of the pride in their own hearts. Pride is an ingredient that should never be introduced into the kitchen. Pride is always a roadblock to the life we are meant to live. It is pride that keeps you from being open to the truth, it is pride that closes doors, and pride that causes trouble and heartache for those who won't let it go. When The Master Chef searches the heart, He is searching for those who can set themselves aside, surrendering daily to His will, in order that He may do His greatest work through you. Having pride in your heart is like trying to stir a pot without a spoon.

"Just look at the examples in the Bible. In spite of His

greater knowledge and purpose, Christ never held Himself up higher than the people to whom He was witnessing. He lovingly reached out to those that the worldly leaders disapproved of. He humbly went to a painful death on the cross, surrendering His life for us, so that by His sacrifice, we can have salvation.

"We too should have that same humble attitude, removing pride, and striving for unity with Him. Search with an open, humble heart, a desire to change and a willingness to learn. The Master Chef has a purpose for you, which is far greater than you could ever imagine.

"As you learn to walk with Him, don't give up. When challenges arise, and they will, be persistent. Wherever you find a stumbling block, let your faith turn it into a stepping stone. As you read, study and pray, The Master Chef will be right there to guide you."

"This sounds more like a Bible study that it does a restaurant pep talk," Lisa said.

"Well, it's both," Phil said. "We want all of us to be healthier as a family. Healthier physically, healthier mentally and definitely healthier spiritually."

"I actually like the thought of Bible studies," Steve said.

"That's a totally great idea," Sally agreed.

"We might have to do that some night," Mike said. "I realize I may be sounding a little preachy here, but I have a passion for serving the Lord and I have a passion to see every single one of you serve Him as well. The prep room seems to be my office for now, and I'm here for all of you anytime. Thank you all for coming. I think we are done here for today, Phil."

"Yes we are, so we will see you all Monday. Have a great weekend with your families," Phil concluded.

Phil, Mike and Jenny rose to leave, but quickly realized that no one else did.

"Is there something else?" Phil asked.

"I'd like to know more about The Master Chef," Eric said.

"Me too," Edith agreed.

"Yeah, like has God literally talked to you for real?" Sally asked.

"Will you please tell us more?" Lisa encouraged.

"Well... Okay, but if anyone needs to go, please do. I don't want to keep you from anything," Mike said returning to his seat. No one made a move to leave, so Mike smiled and continued his message.

"Let me give you a crash course on the relationship," Mike said. "The relationship with The Master Chef actually starts long before we ever enter into the kingdom's kitchen. It all begins with the interviewing process. Questions asked, questions answered. The Master Chef wants you in His kingdom, but the question is, do you really want to be there? It's not always the one with the most experience that gets the job. Far too often people have been doing things their own way for so many years that they are unwilling to change their ways and learn the ways of The Master Chef. He chooses those who are the most willing to learn. These are the ones that are easier to train the right way rather than trying to retrain those who are unwilling to change poor habits. Fortunately for us, The Master Chef is willing to accept every single one of us exactly as we are. After all, who knows us better than anyone else?"

"The Master Chef of all the universe?" Kimmie answered.

"That's right! And he has been cultivating that relationship with us since before we were even born. He has been with us every step of the way, even if we never realized it. Our relationship with Him may feel brand new, but it is really the result of an eternity of planning by a God who loves us beyond reason, and wants nothing more than to be our very best Friend.

"I'll never forget my interview with the Master Chef. He asked me, 'What characteristics do you look for in a good friend?' I was a little surprised because it wasn't a typical question that one would expect to hear in an interview. I thought for a moment and said, 'I look for a trustworthy person that I can share anything and everything with. One who holds the same common core values that I do. And it's nice to have someone who shares the same passions, interests and goals that I do.'

"Several months later, I asked the Master Chef what the significance of that question was. He told me that the question was like a mirror image of the type of person that I would be as a friend to others. 'WOW!' was all I could say. And now, years later, The Master Chef is my best friend, trustworthy and true."

"God really does talk to you?" Lisa asked, amazed.

"Quite often now, but that takes a deep relationship. And not something most people can accept or understand."

"So you actually have open dialogue with God?" Steve asked.

"Not always," Mike answered. "Most of the time I talk and He listens. Sometimes He sends me deep impressions by the Holy Spirit. And then other times it is a literal voice. But it's always exactly what I need in that moment. Now, back to you. You are still interviewing, so be sharp. You never know what questions The Master Chef is going to ask you. You may have to dig deep into your heart to find the answers. Just be honest, and everything will be fine.

"It's easy to forget that The Master Chef knows us better than we know ourselves. Quite often we find ourselves struggling with our issues, justifying our reasons to continue in our own ways, rather than realizing that His ways are so much better. But as your relationship grows, you will come to trust Him with your life, and that's when the real change begins. And you will never forget the moment when The Master Chef says, 'You got the job!' Remember when you got your first job? You were on the phone one minute later calling everybody to share your excitement. How many of you are that excited about being a child of God? How many of you are that enthusiastic about working for The Master

Chef of the entire universe?"

As Mike looked around the room, it was apparent that no one had really experienced the true exhilaration of knowing God. "See!" Mike said, shaking his head. "We have a long way to go to develop that relationship and find real joy in Him."

Mike continued, "Now, before you begin a worldly job, you first have to go through the new hire process with human resources. There is all the paperwork to complete and the policies to become familiar with. When you work for The Master Chef, the Bible is your employee handbook, so you know what is involved in working in the kingdom's kitchen.

"You may be surprised to learn that when you start working for The Master Chef, there won't be any contract to sign. He will ask for a commitment all right, but until you are ready to enter into a covenant relationship with Him, then you won't be hired. Your commitment must be so strong that any type of contractual agreement on paper is meaningless compared to a covenant.

"In many new jobs, you would expect some sort of orientation session. And in larger organizations, you might go through several classes before setting foot into an actual workstation. The Master Chef could have a dozen workstations just in the main food service area, and possibly hundreds of workstations throughout the kingdom's kitchens. But your job is to first learn the station that you have been hired for. In time, you may start learning other stations; that all depends on how you use your skills. You will have unlimited potential to become proficient at any position available. Psalm 75:6-7 says, 'promotion comes not from the east, nor from the west, nor from the south. But God is the judge: and he can put down one, and promote up another.'

"As you start your first days of actual on hands training, you may be shadowing someone, watching what they are doing, seeing how they are doing it, and allowing your brain to absorb information without having any to perform the actual tasks yet."

"That's what you did with me on the line that first day." Eddie said.

"Yes I did, and one of the best things you can do in your spiritual walk is find people who really know the Bible, and shadow them. Although you should never accept everything someone teaches without making sure that it is biblically correct, this is part of the process of learning. And do understand that everybody makes mistakes, even the people you are shadowing. But because The Master Chef is involved in every aspect of His kitchen, rest assured that you are in good hands; trial and error is part of the process. Making mistakes is okay as long as you maintain an attitude of humility and learn from your mistakes.

"Then comes the day when you are on your own. You have gone through the whole process of interviewing, all the orientation, the training, and now it's your time to shine. You have a covenant relationship with The Master Chef and He is looking for you to use the knowledge you have acquired.

"Your adrenaline is flowing with excitement and anticipation, wanting so desperately to impress The Master

Chef. If only we were all this excited to be serving the Lord every day.

"The orders start coming in. The Master Chef is quick to look at your creations to ensure that they are up to His standards. He may make some adjustments, or glance through your station to see how organized or sloppy you are. You continue to focus on the work at hand until He catches your eye and gives you a nod of approval for a job well done. And your heart is overwhelmed with joy that The Master Chef is pleased with you!"

"I've been there!" Eddie shouted. "Just recently."

"That's right, both Eddie and Eric were dishwashing. Now they're on the front line, and their food is looking great!" Mike smiled and the beaming brothers and continued.

"In time, as your relationship with The Master Chef grows, you become more competent in your position. Your trust in Him grows stronger and your bond strengthens until The Master Chef has such confidence in you that He is ready to begin training you for other stations.

"Regardless of what position The Master Chef puts you in, you will still need to find balance to keep from getting overwhelmed, and that's why He created a Sabbath day of rest. On this day, The Master Chef sets all the work aside; all the worries and stress that the world seems to pressure people with are gone. Sabbath is a day to praise and worship the One whom we love to serve."

"Amen!" Kimmie shouted, then giggled. "That really is so

much fun to say!"

"Well, I think that's enough for tonight," Mike chuckled. We can continue another time. Goodnight, everyone."

Jenny and Phil stayed behind to talk with Mike and Steve and discuss a game plan for how to accomplish the new to-do list.

"What are we going to do about these new menus?" Phil asked. "Right now, breakfast is rocking and lunch is still average, with dinner pulling up the end."

Steve nodded. "Dinner never has been our claim to fame, and closing at 7:00 is too early to attract a real dinner crowd."

"I agree with Steve," Mike said.

"We need to expand our hours and change the menu from burgers and sandwiches to real dinner entrees," Steve said.

"There is no doubt about that; we definitely need to raise the bar," Phil agreed.

"The problem with that is this atmosphere. We're not a gourmet restaurant," Jenny commented. "Look around; this is a country cooking feel at best."

Phil sighed. "Jenny's right, guys. But for us to do a remodel, it would take thousands of dollars, many hours of remodeling, and we run the risk of losing the atmosphere that draws people in here for breakfast and lunch."

"Steve," Mike asked, "what are the best-selling restaurant items in this area?"

"I'd say it's probably catfish and ribeye steaks."

"So not the filet mignon, not the shrimp scampi, not the prime rib? Would all of you agree?" Mike asked.

Phil, Jenny and Steve nodded in agreement.

"So, do we want to be like them, or do we want to be better, different?"

"Better, definitely better." Phil said.

"I like the idea of something different, too," Jenny added.

"Both!" Steve said emphatically.

"Exactly," Mike said. "So let's start by assuming that this is really not the place you're going to dine at if you're trying to impress a date on a Saturday night, right?"

"Right," the others agreed.

"So, what we need to do first is create a dinner menu that really draws regular people in for our country hospitality," Mike said.

"And I think staying open until 9:00pm would be great," Steve added.

"A lot of the restaurants around here are open until 11:00," Mike said.

"I think we ought to let those places fight for the crumbs," Phil decided. "Let's just focus on the 5 to 8 pm crowd. And if people really want to eat here, they'll know our hours and come when we're open."

"I'll mock up a new menu this weekend for all of you to look at and approve," Mike said. "We can start the new hours on Monday."

"Sounds good to me," Steve said. "And since it will be slow at night these first few weeks, get me a can of paint, and I can start on our new look."

"Great! See you tomorrow," Phil said as they headed for the door. "Thank you Lord, for a great meeting."

"Amen!"

By the time Phil and Jenny got home, they were absolutely exhausted. Fortunately, they didn't have to go to work Saturday morning. They were taking their very first step toward obeying God's commandments. Never again would they put the worldly work in front of the Sabbath day that God set aside for worship. But they were not doing it in order to earn salvation; they obeyed simply because of their newly deepened love for Christ.

We've got Reception

…>>… Phil awoke the morning after the earthquake, dreaming of that first employee meeting of years long past. His sleepy fog quickly wore off as he realized that they were in the trailer and the tragedies from the earthquake were still right outside the door. He knelt by his bed to pray, as he was so accustomed to doing. His thoughts centered on his loved ones as he prayed for their protection.

"I've got it!" Phil said suddenly, waking Jenny.

"Got it? Got what?"

"An idea. We have the new generator and the satellite dish."

"*Yes*, we do! Can you get that thing to work?" Jenny asked.

"I'll work on that, if you work on some breakfast?" Phil suggested.

"Sounds good to me," Jenny said. "I'm going to have to go through the fridge in the house this morning and get what I can into this little refrigerator."

"I'll make sure the propane is working on this fridge too," Phil replied.

Phil checked the propane on the fridge and then began fiddling with the satellite. After an hour, he started getting some reception.

"Honey Bear, you're getting something!" Jenny shouted out the trailer door. "And breakfast is ready!"

Entering the trailer, Phil saw the table set up with a plate of fresh fruit and a bowl of steaming oatmeal. "I've got the satellite pointed at the exact degree it's supposed to be, but the barn might be in the way a little bit."

Sitting down for breakfast, Jenny prayed, "Lord, we thank You for this day, and thank You for Your protection throughout the times to come. Bless this food to strengthen us and give us the energy to get through the day. In Jesus' name, Amen."

"Amen. This looks great," Phil said.

"Best I can do today. We're going to have to eat all this refrigerated food within the next couple of days, and I'm guessing that the frozen food in the kitchen won't last long either. Then there is the freezer in the garage, and that's got a lot of food in it too."

"I've got the generator out here for the trailer, but it's not going to reach the freezer too, so we'll have to move either the freezer or the trailer," Phil said.

"I think we need to stay back here," Jenny said.

"I agree. Do we have some cords?" Phil asked.

"Just down at the restaurant," Jenny replied.

Flipping through the channels, it was just one "No Reception" message after another.

"Where are the channels?" Jenny asked, "I thought I saw one earlier."

"Yeah, it's a recorded program, nothing live," Phil said. Tapping through a couple more satellite buttons, he finally found a live news broadcast. "Here we go." The studio set looked like it had sustained some damage, yet they were still broadcasting. "Let's Listen."

Turning up the volume, they heard the broadcaster announce, "Again, for those in need of assistance, it will likely not be available for quite some time. All power systems are shut down and emergency back-up systems will most likely also be disappearing soon. Those with generators who are receiving these signals are advised to share this information with others and conserve their generators' power in order to be able to receive further updates."

"Look Honey Bear, down below," Jenny said. "There are notices of where to tune."

Phil grabbed a pen and began writing. "Sat Com 14 62* north west." Phil wrote down every suggested communication avenue they had.

"Everyone is advised to remain in your homes or attempt to reach a designated shelter in your area. Many churches and convention centers have been converted to public shelters. Here is a list of nearby shelter locations."

"Salt Lake City? This is a Salt Lake City broadcast!" Phil exclaimed. "How big is this problem?"

Phil flipped through the channels in search of another station, but couldn't get anything.

"I need to move the dish," Phil said. "Watch sweetheart, and let me know what you see."

After a minute Jenny shouted, "There, right there! Don't move it."

Coming inside, Phil could hear a British accent and assumed they had tuned in to the BBC. "Damages are global, but may not be as bad as we first reported. There are massive tsunamis throughout the world, though most are not as serious as those which wiped out the U.S. State of Florida and the Philippines. Those seem to be the global high points. Earthquake tremors are still believed to be numbered into the thousands per day, but with no power to many areas, we cannot confirm results."

"Oh Phil, look how global this problem is! I had no idea," Jenny said.

"Regardless of where you are, the UN has advised that everyone connect and communicate with others. Your nearest neighbors are the first line of contact, and any civil authorities you can locate. Many cities have already reported systems of communications and a degree of order, while others are still in a state of chaos."

"Mike said things like this would happen," Phil said.

"He sure did," Jenny replied.

"Well, we can sit here and go batty looking at this stuff, or we can head to town and see what we can do," Phil said.

"What we can do?" There's nothing *to* do. I say we just stay here for a few days and let everyone else go crazy out there."

"We need to at least go down to the restaurant," Phil said. "There may be people there needing us."

"I do agree with that," Jenny replied. "It's only a few miles, and if we can't make it all the way in, which is a good possibility, we can just turn around and come back."

"We need to try to fill the truck with food, too," Phil said. "Plus, I guarantee people are going to show up there."

"Well, let's just leave everything here and powered down for now."

Jenny and Phil drove the truck up to the side door of the garage, and Phil carefully entered the half-collapsed house. After a few minutes, Phil emerged with a couple of pistols and a shotgun over his shoulder.

"Do you really need those guns?" Jenny asked.

"Probably not, but we never know what desperate or evil people we might run into."

"Yeah, who also have guns," Jenny nervously replied.

Zigzagging between downed power poles and trees, it took well over an hour to get to the restaurant. When they arrived, there were strangers carrying out boxes of food. Inside, Lisa and Steve were sitting in a booth. Steve too had a pistol strapped to his side.

"Number one!" Phil said as Steve stood up to hug him.

"I knew you were going to be here today," Steve said.

"Anybody else show up here? Phil asked.

"Joy and her husband Rick were here with their two kids, and said they'd be back later. The brothers are in the kitchen cleaning up."

"Eddie! Eric!" Phil shouted.

The brothers came out of the kitchen and embraced Phil joyfully.

"What in the world are you two doing in there?"

"Just boxing up perishables for the hungry," Eric replied.

"Yeah," Eddie added, "rather than fighting with them, we give it to them just like Mike taught us, and we have had nothing but appreciation instead of a fight."

Phil smiled. "You guys are so smart."

Jenny's observant gaze fell to the boys' clothing, then to Steve and Lisa in the booth. "Wait a minute, you guys are all still in uniform. You've been here since your shifts yesterday, haven't you?"

"Yes we have," Steve replied. "We prayed about it and God impressed us to stay here. We took turns napping in the office. The building itself really didn't get much damage."

"The steel frame and roof are holding together pretty well," Phil said. "Our steel pole barn held up too."

Suddenly, Jenny's eyes filled with worry and darted frantically around the restaurant. "Where's Mickey?"

"It's OK Jenny, he's sleeping in the office," Lisa reassured her. "We picked him up from school yesterday and brought him here, praise God. My sister was going to pick him up, but then the quake hit."

"What about the gas lines?" Phil asked.

"Well there's no gas coming out of them, so there must be a break somewhere," Steve said. "I did shut off the main."

"And the food?" Jenny asked.

"All the small coolers have been emptied, and we are going through the bigger coolers now," Lisa said.

Steve turned to Phil and asked, "What are we going to do, Captain?"

"Well, Mike said at this time we need to stick together, and since our place is the farthest out of town, I would suggest that we all get out there and set up camp. Why don't you go home and grab everything you need. Is your car running?"

"It should be, there are no trees on it," Steve laughed.

"In fact, take Eddie with you and go by their place too. Pack everything you can and get back here ASAP. We will wait here until 6:00p.m., then we'll have to head back. It's best if you follow us through the maze of downed power lines. We can't take chances driving alone in the dark."

"We'll take over here," Jenny offered.

"Sounds good. Come on Eddie, let's get going." Steve and Eddie hurried out the door.

As they were leaving, Phil shouted, "Bring sleeping bags and beds too! Just strap them to the roof!"

Just then, a couple of kids came into the restaurant.

"Hello," Steve said. "Do you need some food?"

"Yes, we, we do. We - we need..." The startled pair stammered, their faces fearful.

"Come here kids," Lisa said, directing them into the dark kitchen. "Do you have a family that needs food?"

"Yes, we do."

The kids came out with a large box of assorted foods, almost too big to carry.

Throughout the day, dozens of people came in to get boxes of food. Phil backed the truck up to the back door and Eric helped fill it with dry goods and non-perishables. They also packed the catering truck, which held many cases of food and supplies. They were even grabbing pots and pans, cutting boards; whatever they could take was packed. But the freezer was the big issue.

By the end of the day, every single employee had made it down to the restaurant. Phil informed them of what was going on globally and advised them all to come out to the house. Some wanted to stay and others were leaning toward going to the shelters. The employees who had heard Mike's messages knew they needed to get out of town.

Steve and Eddie returned with another truck, and Phil had them pack the entire freezer's worth of food into it and the van. It was time to go, and with everyone informed of the destination, the caravan journeyed back to the house.

Once they got to the house, the real work began. The kitchen and patio were commandeered by Steve and Lisa with little Mickey. Eddie and Eric wanted to try to fix a place in the partially collapsed garage. Joy and Rick got to work renovating the barn to accommodate the others.

Phil called all the men together to establish a plan of action. Although the core of the house was collapsed, they still needed to retrieve necessities.

"I think what we need to do is demo the damaged areas of the house and see where we can access the main structure. We need to get beds, blankets, towels - anything we can use. I've got a chainsaw here, so let's dig in. And be careful!" Phil was taking charge just as if he was at the restaurant.

"I think with all this food, we need to see if we can get your kitchen refrigerator moved to the barn first, then the ladies can start packing it," Rick suggested.

"And we saw a freezer in the garage," Eddie added.

"There are actually two of them," Phil said. "That's a great idea. But we don't have a lot of time. It will be dark in a couple of hours, so we need to work quick. Let's start a wood pile over by the trailer and use a lot of this busted up house to burn until we can chop up firewood."

"My kids are old enough to start stacking," Rick said.

"Mickey can help too," Steve added.

The pole barn didn't sustain any damage to the steel framing and was an ideal place to stockpile the food and supplies. While the men were busy digging through debris, the ladies set up their temporary homes.

Before darkness fell, everyone was settled in and secure enough to get through the night. They managed to get the kitchen fridge and the garage freezers out to the barn and plugged into the generator. Frozen foods were packed into the freezers with not an inch to spare. The rest of the perishable food was stacked in the pole barn with the frozen foods on the cool concrete, topped by the remains of the refrigerated foods. A tarp was stretched over the stack to keep it all cool, but the food would only be useable for a couple of days. The food supply was plentiful for now, but with twelve people to feed and possibly more coming, it wasn't going to last for long.

Abby, Megan and Mickey did a great job of creating a wood stock that would last for days, while Steve built a campfire in the cinderblock burn pit a few yards away from the trailer. It was actually a decent camp setup, with plenty of chairs around the fire for everyone and a couple of sturdy tables for food service.

The ladies had prepared a feast of perishable leftovers that would not make it through the night and everyone gathered together at the trailer where Phil had connected the television to the outside port. The crackling sounds of a roaring fire helped to soothe the mounting tension.

Once the group was seated, Phil bowed his head to pray. "Lord we thank You for gathering us all together once again. It is a different circumstance this time, but we know that Your love for us never changes. Bless this meal, and be with us in these days of confusion, directing us to the Rock of our salvation. In Jesus' name, Amen."

"Amen."

"Do you all want to watch the news?" Phil asked. "We were able to get BBC News on the satellite dish earlier."

I also have The Waltons on DVD," Jenny said.

"The Waltons!" the kids all shouted in unison.

"We really need to find out what's happening. We'd better watch the news," Steve suggested. The other adults agreed.

"Well kids, you've been out voted, so we'll have to watch the Waltons tomorrow," Jenny said. "Let's listen to the news."

The BBC was still running 24-hour coverage of the global situation. "The world is in turmoil, and there seems to be no end in sight. As of today, all nations have called all emergency personnel to service. Active and inactive military have been called to their posts. In the United States, the National Guard has been activated in every state." The broadcaster drew his hand to his ear to receive incoming data. "This just in; here are pictures of the nuclear plant in Beijing China, where the entire reactor is in a meltdown. These photos are from 20 miles away, and you can see the plume of smoke. Evacuations are inevitable. Again, if you are not in need of emergency services, the UN has advised that everyone remain at home, or find a shelter in your area. Connecting with neighbors is strongly advised. We now take you to Rome, where the Pope is addressing the world."

The Pope stood to speak, his message voiced-over by an on-air translator.

"My dear children, I come before you as we stand in this time of global turmoil, with catastrophe striking every corner of the earth. It is a time of confusion, suffering and fear. Not only are we faced with unthinkable natural disaster, but our world is also a place of increasing conflict, with violence, hatred and brutal atrocities committed continually, even in the name of religion. I am, as are so many of you, deeply worried by the disturbing natural, social and political crises taking place today.

"The two main questions we must ask at this time are 'Why is this happening?' and 'What shall we do?' Those answers exist, but they cannot be sought without a humble willingness to surrender our preconceived ideas and beliefs and a willingness to come together and join with our fellow man for the greater good.

"To answer the first question, my dear ones, this world is being cursed by our God, whose patience, liberty and hopeful sorrow has reached its limit. He can no longer allow us to destroy this earth and one another under the banner of freedom, and is calling us to return to Him, that we might be blessed.

"We have, for centuries, disregarded the sacred traditions of God and attempted to interpret His will for ourselves. We have turned away from His appointed representatives, and blindly obeyed the dictates of our own consciences. Our arrogance has known no bounds, and we have caused the breakdown of our planet and the destruction of our virtue.

"As to the second question, we must remain calm, but we must also act decisively. It is time to cease our vain independence and submit to divine authority. We must resist the temptation to assert our individual rights and seek personal gain above global preservation. It is easy to react to such widespread crisis by thinking only of ourselves, but our response must instead be one of hope and healing, of peace and justice. We must move forward together, as one, in a renewed spirit of unity, solidarity and cooperation. The challenges facing us today call for serious and definite action. The solutions to our problems require love of the common good and a spirit of solidarity. We need to be holy, we need to be pure, we need to be united in repentance. God's healing of our world is conditional to our actions. Brotherly love is a necessity. It is time for all of us to come together and put our religious differences aside. This is not the time to fight, this is the time to repent and return to the Lord. All people, of all faiths - Christians, Muslims, Buddhists, Jews, Atheists and all others must unite for the benefit of all mankind. We must do this to survive as individual nations. We must do this to survive as a human race.

"Please, my beloved, I beseech you to join with me in returning to our God so that we may assuage His wrath and save our world. May God be with us all."

The pontiff raised his arms and invited the crowd to join him in reciting the Lord's Prayer. As the multitude began to speak, thick, dark clouds began drawing together overhead. A faint, rumbling sound began in the distance then grew louder, until the voices of the assembly were nearly drowned out by the roar. The ground trembled and everyone feared another earthquake was about to hit, but the Pope's gaze never wavered from the sky. His face held an expression of gentle peace as he spoke the words, "For Thine is the kingdom, and the power, and the glory forever and ever. Amen."

The very moment the last word left his lips, a bolt of lightning lit up the black sky over the Holy Father's head, and a ball of fire struck the ground then shot up into a pillar, blazing with an almost blinding light. The bright flame flashed brilliantly and then disappeared, leaving a patch of charred, blackened concrete in the shape of a cross on the dais where the Pope stood.

The crowd stood in stunned silence for several seconds, then erupted in deafening cheers. The Pope continued to stand with his arms raised, tears streaming down his cheeks. "My children, will you not hear the voice of our God? Will you not return to Him?" He implored the onlookers as they continued to cheer, many weeping and praying aloud.

The television shot switched back to the BBC studio, where a stunned reporter began a stammering commentary. Phil stood and switched off the television set, his face ashen.

"Wow!" Steve gasped, breaking the shocked silence.

"Yeah, can you believe that?" Kimmie said. "That's exactly the way Mike said it would happen."

"Calling for differences to be put aside," Jenny said, shaking her head. "The wounds being healed, just like the Bible said."

"Signs and wonders…" Phil said quietly, shaking his head. He still couldn't believe what he had just seen.

"False wonders," Steve added. "That was Revelation 13, verses 12-14 in action. There's no way that fire was the work of God."

"I'm surprised the Pope didn't call for Sunday to be made an official worldwide day of rest. He has been suggesting that for years now," Rick said.

"I remember back just a couple of years ago, when the Pope was talking about Sunday needing to be a family day," Phil recalled. "He never did mention it as a commandment of God."

"Yes, I remember that too," Edith said. "Looking back, it seems like people were initially lured into the Sunday-keeping mentality for worldly purposes, not godly reasons."

"I totally remember Mike saying something like… First the power of something…?" Sally's voice drifted as she tried to remember Mike's words.

"It's first the power of persuasion, then persuasion by power," Steve said. He knew the truth of those words only too well.

"Well, let's just hunker down and…" Phil hesitated, then brightened. "Let's sing some songs!"

"When we all get to heaven, what a day of rejoicing that will be!" Jenny sang,
the others joining in. "When we all see Jesus, we'll sing and shout the victory."

The song brought such comfort that the group stayed up singing songs and reminiscing until midnight. Everyone reminisced about the things Mike taught them about biblical prophecy and events to come. Now they found joy in the realization that these things were at last coming to pass.

"I miss Mike," Steve said. "I really loved him."

"Me too," Lisa agreed.

"Yeah, he just had a way about him," Jenny added. "Do you guys remember when we were singing 'Beloved, let us love one another…?'"

"Oh yes, that was at the opening of the Ultimate Buffet he created for Sundays," Edith remembered.

"That's right, Sunday morning. I remember," Beth added. "That was when he decided to do all those huddle times with messages. I loved his Bible studies."

"I remember it like it was yesterday," Phil said. "He quoted Julia Child saying, 'Careful cooking is love.'"

Exhaustion from the hard work of the day finally caught up with them, and everyone headed off to their makeshift beds. Steve and Lisa cuddled up together on the couch, with little Mickey fast asleep on the reclining chair. Phil loaded up the fire to help it burn through the night, pulled a blanket over Mickey, and whispered good night to the dozing couple. As Steve drifted off to sleep, his thoughts wandered back to the day of the Ultimate Buffet's grand opening.

The Ultimate Buffet

…<<… "Welcome everyone," Mike said. "Today's the day. We're about to unveil the Ultimate Buffet to the community at large. I'm so glad you could all get here early for prayer; we have a big day ahead of us and we definitely need to pray. We've spent weeks getting the entire restaurant ready - remodeling the bathrooms, painting, and adding that exterior brick to the front of the restaurant. That certainly was a job wasn't it Phil?"

"It sure was," Phil replied.

"And by the way everyone, Phil has now lost 40 pounds since his heart attack just a few short months ago."

Everyone applauded and cheered so loud that even the people lined up outside waiting for the restaurant to open could hear them.

"Julia Child once said, 'I think careful cooking is love, don't you?' I believe that what we need to do is consume the love of The Master Chef, who gave us the talent to produce this wonderful experience for the community."

"Okay!" Mike said, caught his breath and studied the sheet of paper on his clipboard. "Speech time. The thing we need to remember is that the tasks that we are doing here today are not for our benefit, but rather for the glory of The Master Chef. It's our job to please Him in everything we do. When we serve Him out of love, it's easy to do a better job. Are you going to get the job done faster? Not always, but it will be done better. Faster is not always better. Some things need to be put in the slow cooker. Dehydration, a form of preservation, takes time, just like witnessing to those who have never heard of The Master Chef's unconditional love takes time.

"It's not the love we have for the things we do or the love for the materialistic elements of life that bring the greatest satisfaction. The love we have for each other and the love we share with The Master Chef surpass all others. Godly love should be the basis for all we do, and when we spread that love to the people around us, it can be quite contagious.

"We often see the heroic actions of a person risking their life to save another, and most of us would do whatever we could to save the life of someone in need. Is this done out of love? Or is this just basic human instinct? It probably is, to a certain extent, but the greater the risk, the less one will do to save another. But The Master Chef loves us so much that He was willing to die for us. In His selfless act of love, there was no hesitation in the face of His inevitable death in order to save sinners. If you truly knew it was going to cost your life, with no possibility whatsoever of survival, would you still be willing to die for that stranger on the street? It would take an incredible love to do that even for someone you really care about. Most of us wouldn't be willing to give up our lives to save another, but that's exactly what The Master Chef did.

"The enemy has persistently tried to twist and destroy our understanding of God's love for us, but it remains the same - constant, unconditional, and beyond any power we could ever comprehend. Indeed, love is the power source in The Master Chef's kitchen that enables us to serve with passion. The greater we experience The Master Chef's love for us, the greater our passion to serve Him well. An infusion of genuine, selfless love produces perfect results every time.

"Love is the most powerful force in the universe. It is The Master Chef's love for us that enables us to receive His priceless, undeserved grace. It is love that makes possible our forgiveness and salvation. It is an understanding of His love that enables us to truly give and receive real love in a way we've never been able to before.

"How many of us have ever had an earthly boss who gave unconditional love?" Mike said, motioning to Phil. "How many of us ever had a boss that *loved* us, even a little? It is very rare for a boss to show any real love for the team, let alone a love so true that they would be willing to lay down their very life, like The Master Chef did for every single one of His team members.

"The Master Chef's love is deep and true, and it's this love that gives us the comfort and confidence to know that we can trust Him in everything He does and everything He asks of us. What a love The Master Chef has for us! Love that provides protection, comfort and peace, and would never do us harm. His love is like no other.

"You have accepted a position working for The Master Chef of the entire universe. Today, we are in His hands, and we all need to work together with a higher purpose in mind. Set self aside so that production can remain at its best and highest.

"The job you have been waiting for your entire life is right here. A job that you love, working for a Master Chef who truly loves you. It really does sound like a bunch of fluffy white bunnies, a fairytale that could never happen, but the fact of the matter is that it's all real. Don't get me wrong, there will be challenges and struggles. You may even be faced with situations in which you have no idea what to do or how to do it. But with The Master Chef working right by your side, rest assured that His love will guide you through any struggle and help you to find your true passion in life. Now, being a chef myself, one of my great passions is food. By serving The Master Chef, I've learned more about food than I ever would have without Him. Just look at all of the wonderful foods that He has created for us! So on that note, please follow me into the Ultimate Buffet and let's get started."

As everyone entered the banquet room for the first time in weeks, they were all shocked by the remarkable transformation. Jenny crossed the room and turned on the background music planned to enhance the dining experience. The seating had been increased for an additional one-hundred and fifty people. All along the right side of the room, the enormous buffet was spread out in breathtaking array with stations for everything imaginable.

The first station was a live omelet station where people could create their own omelette and egg creations. Eric took his place behind the station to simulate the concept for everyone. Next to that was a hot buffet station with different types of potatoes, hash browns, pancakes, french toast and waffles with a full-blown topping station.

Then there was a circular station of chilled foods with an ice sculpture swan centerpiece. To one side of the swan were dozens of different fruits, and on the other side were salads of every variety. The far side of the buffet mirrored the breakfast side, but was filled with dinner items. Baked chicken, sea bass smothered with a light champagne sauce, and vegan meatloaf with potatoes of every sort and ten different types of carefully prepared vegetables.

The highlight of the buffet was a live carving station. It was Eddie's station for the day, so he took his place and prepared to carve whole roasted turkeys and prime rib. Mike had thought of every detail, right down to the placement of the au jus, accompanied by whipped cream horseradish and cranberry chiffon.

On the end of the massive buffet was a fresh soup and bread station containing a dozen different breads and five crocks of hometown soup favorites. The final station nestled on the far wall was a dessert station with sweet treats of every kind.

After all the employees were escorted through the buffet, Mike gathered them together for prayer. "May you be filled with the love of The Master Chef, and may His love flow out of you to everyone around you. May you be filled with gratitude for all of the wonderful creations that The Master Chef has given us, and for the countless miracles and blessings we receive every day. May you always have the greatest love for the Creator of the universe, Who loved us first, and Who will always love us. Amen."

"AMEN!" Everyone echoed.

"1 John 3:1, 'Behold, what manner of love the Father has given unto us, that we should become the sons of God.' Everybody sing!"

Everyone joined the singing in a moment to never be forgotten.

"Behold, what manner of love the Father has given unto

us…"

"OK, stations, everybody," Mike called out. "We're opening the doors!"

Over thirty people waited in line outside the restaurant doors, including the mayor and a reporter and photographer from local newspaper. Mike unlocked the door and told the crowd, "It's only 7:40, but we're going to open a little early for you."

As the patrons streamed in, Mike greeted the mayor and the newspaper team, who began photographing the buffet spread before the customers dug into the beautifully arranged food.

Everyone was absolutely speechless at what the buffet had to offer. There wasn't a disappointed taste bud in the house that day. The line stretched out the door for the majority of the day, but moved quickly, and the customers enthusiastically proclaimed the food well worth the wait. With the vast array of high quality food and beautiful presentation, no one even flinched at the $15.99 price.

At day's end, when the last dish was washed and the lights went down, Lisa and Steve met in the office with Mike, Phil and Jenny.

"Well?" Steve asked.

"Well what?" Phil teasingly replied.

"How did we do? Come on, we're waiting," Lisa said.

Jenny, who was still crunching the final numbers, said "It looks like we did 1,300 covers."

"*Wow!*" Are you serious?" Steve's eyes widened in surprise.

"Actually," Jenny continued, "we need to add the 230 kids' meals too. And if you count the under-five year-olds who eat free, we've done over 1,500 covers."

"And then there are the dozen or so comps today for the VIP crowd," Phil added.

My guess is this won't be the normal turnout," Mike said. "I would estimate that a 30% reduction would be reasonable. We should average about a thousand covers each Sunday."

Mike leaned over to Phil and whispered in his ear, "You just had a twenty-thousand dollar day." Then, in response to the huge smile stealing across Phil's face, he added, "You're gonna have to hire more help."

"So Lisa, how did you do in tips today?" Phil asked the head waitress.

"Well, I did over three-hundred dollars," Lisa replied humbly, not wanting to boast, but clearly excited.

"Wow! That's fantastic!" Jenny exclaimed.

"See," Phil said, "that's what I was looking for. Because with money like that, we can really make sure that we've got the best team working here."

"And keep them too," Lisa added. "But that number's not even counting the tips I gave to the bus boys and kitchen team."

"Really? You tipped the kitchen staff?" Phil asked.

"Oh yeah," Mike said, "I told the servers to tip the bus boys 10%, and another 10% to the kitchen staff, since the servers are really handling two times the tables but having half the work because of the rest of the team."

"Well I think that's terrific," Phil said. "Great job everyone."

The buffet became a community favorite, with a full house every Sunday. The numbers never did drop off as Mike had anticipated. After a few months of consistent results, the restaurant had definitely forged a new image. Operations were as smooth as could be, the team was well trained and well paid, and the restaurant staff had low turnover and high demand for employment. It was like a dream for Jenny and Phil, who finally felt that their work was paying off after so many years.

The banquet room was only used on Sundays and a little bit of overflow for the restaurant during lunches which, with the new menus, eventually surpassed breakfast in sales. Dinner was still dragging along with some increases, but with the lack of housing in the area, Phil knew it would be years before that shift would grow. On weekdays, many of the construction firms in the area would meet in the banquet rooms for extended meetings. Overall, the little greasy spoon diner was now transformed into a well tuned, healthy option country cafe.

Sabbath Service

One Saturday morning, all of the employees received a call to meet at the restaurant, and encouraged to bring their friends and families for a surprise event. No one knew what they were in for, they just knew not to be late. As people began showing up, they were confronted by locked doors and a sign with an arrow that read "Private Celebration - Use Side Door."

Inside the banquet room, music was playing. Steve was playing his guitar while the others sang hymns and gospel song. Song after song, their hearts were captivated as they lifted their voices in praise. Mike had stapled pages of printed lyrics for everyone to follow along with. As the last notes of the final song ended and everyone was seated, Mike stood up in the front of the room and began to preach.

"Father God," Mike prayed, "be with us on this Sabbath day, as we gather in Your holy name. Bless this day that You have set aside for us to draw ever closer to You. We are wholly Yours; be with me as I speak Your words, in Jesus' name. Amen."

"I thank you all for coming today for what is to be a day of fellowship, a day to praise the Lord who has given us life, who has given us talent and purpose to do His will. Just about six months ago, I came here at the urging of the Lord. I thought I was here to help Phil lose weight and get healthy, *and he has!*" Mike exclaimed.

"Sixty pounds!" Phil shouted and shook his belly, getting laughs from everyone.

"With only one hundred to go," Mike smiled, bringing him back to reality.

"I have spoken to most of you about the Sabbath and how its observance has slowly eroded over time through Satan's deception, and eventually overshadowed by Sunday worship. Most people have no idea that Sunday is the Pagan sun worship day. And as I'm sure you know, there really is no disputing God's never-changing Sabbath day. As we have studied many times, the Sabbath begins at sunset on Friday and ends at sunset on Saturday. And since there really isn't any church holding Sabbath services in this community, I thought that we would meet here today. There are millions of Christians around the world who gather together to worship God each Sabbath morning, just as we are today. And in the eleventh hour, when troubles and fear are everywhere; people will be worshiping in garages, caves, barns, and private hiding places."

"And in restaurants!" Eddie said, chuckling.

"Amen!" A chorus of voices affirmed.

Mike glanced at the notes on his clipboard. "My message today is about faith and acceptance. In Hebrews 11:1 it says, 'faith is the assurance of those things we hope for as being the proof of the things we do not see'. It is a conviction of the truth being revealed to us by the Holy Spirit. If 1Corinthians 13 is the 'love' chapter, Hebrews 11 would have to be the 'faith' chapter.

"Now, look back at what examples of faith we find in the patriarchs of the Old Testament. A faith far beyond what most people today can comprehend. Who in their right mind would be willing to sacrifice their own child like Abraham did? How did Noah maintain his faith in the coming flood for 120 years while building the ark? These people had a solid faith, grounded in a relationship with the Master Chef of all the universe. By now I'm sure you all know that when I say the Master Chef, I'm talking about God." With more than forty people assembled, Mike wanted be sure to explain his terminology to the newcomers.

"God introduced Himself to *me* as The Master Chef, but He has many names. Judge, Deliverer, great Physician, Bread of Life, and Prince of Peace, to name just a few. But for me, he is the Master Chef.

"The Master Chef is in the business of earning your trust. He will prove Himself over and over, and will never, ever be found untrustworthy. He will not take you beyond your abilities. He certainly stretches us to continue learning and growing, but if you haven't learned how to crack an egg, He will not have you making omelets. Eric over here has progressed to the point where he is making totally awesome omelets. In fact, we might have to promote him to supervisor. As your faith grows and you continue to tap into His unlimited knowledge, you will be progress to creating fantastic dishes under His direction and before you know it, He will have you running entire operations, leading hundreds of people to 'taste and see that the Lord is good.'

"By grace you are saved *through* Faith. Faith grows through action, by acting on your belief. Again, it all comes back to what you do. Faith responds to God's grace, acting on even the smallest measure of faith, which in turn strengthens the faith and causes it to grow. But the catalyst is God's incredible gift of grace.

"I often think of that wonderful song written by Thomas Chisholm, 'Great is Thy Faithfulness,' and it really hits home to think that The Master Chef's faithfulness to us never waivers. But where is our faithfulness to Him? Developing this faith is one of the most important concepts of the Christian life. As with many recipes, it takes time, commitment, and lots of practice to perfect.

"I'll never forget when The Master Chef gave me my first recipe to prepare. It didn't turn out right at all, and He said, 'try it again.' The second time, it turned out a little better, and continued to improve with each attempt. Now, I don't even need to measure any of the ingredients and it still turns out perfect every time.

"Have you ever noticed how, in a relationship, we develop faith in each other? And the same thing happens in our relationship with The Master Chef. My faith is strengthened by persistent and consistent practices; acting on the trust that I have in God and His word. It's the same in the kitchen - persistence and consistency reaps the rewards of perfection. Even the greatest, most sought-after chefs are only the best because they are regularly honing their skills, putting their knowledge into action. So with faith, consistency enables you to establish a solid foundation, and as your faith increases, your ability does too."

The entire group was captivated by Mike's passion. He preached with such heartfelt emotion, as though he were a seasoned evangelist. His voice carried a tone of gentle authority from God, with a strength and compassionate that increased everyone's desire to better know their Savior.

Mike continued, "Plainly put, having faith is simply

believing. God's word says that He has given everyone a measure of faith, so each of us has the capacity to believe in God, even if we aren't aware of it. Even the faintest, tiniest measure of faith can be awakened by the Holy Spirit and transformed into an incredible, life-changing faith through the power of God's word. The Lord says that 'Faith comes by hearing, and hearing from the word of God.' When we believe what the Bible says, our faith increases, prompting us to act on that faith, which in turn causes it to increase even more.

"We know now that faith comes from hearing the Word. We need to understand that one of the definitions of the word 'listen' in the dictionary, is actually 'obedience.' That's right! To listen means to obey. There are a lot of people listening to the Master Chef with their ears, but they're not listening with their actions. We need to be *doing* what He is asking of us. The work we do for the kingdom's kitchen is a direct result of our faith, and let me tell you, the Master Chef knows your faith by your works. 2 James talks about how works complement our faith. We need to act on what God asks us to do.

"A strong faith produces works, and the Master Chef has plenty of work for us to do. So many Christians can talk a good game, but when it comes down to it, there are no works showing the faith they claim to have. That's because *they have no faith*. It's really that simple.

"Faith and works go hand in hand; they complement each other, strengthen each other, and without each other, they both fail.

"Now, don't let all this talk about works cause you to

misunderstand; your faith is not what saves you! Most people think that it is their faith that saves them. After all, the Bible says we are saved by faith, right? Well, if it is only your faith that saves you; then why would you ever need a savior?"

Mike paused and let his words sink in to the group, then continued. "Sometimes in the Bible we see the words 'faith in Christ' and think that's all we need. But if we look at the original translations, we will see that often, it is actually 'faith *of* Christ.' That's right! And it is when we have the faith *of* Christ that we bring a whole new meaning to faith. This is one of the deepest truths that 99% of the population does not understand. It's not *your* faith, it's *His* faith.

"When the Bible says we are 'saved by faith,' it is the saving faith of Christ and the covenant He has with us. That is our saving faith. Even in James 2:14 it says, 'can faith save you?' The answer is 'no.' Only Christ's faith is the saving faith.

"Saying that *my* faith saves me is humanism; the me, me, me mentality so prevalent today. It is a grave misinterpretation, even an outright deception, orchestrated by Satan himself. But when we have faith of *Christ*, we are holding on to God's power, rather than our own. We are trusting that God's covenant with us is something that He will never break, and that *He* is the Author and Finisher of our faith, not us. Are you getting this?" Mike asked. Seeing the understanding nods all around the room, he continued.

"In the kitchen, we need to have the faith of the Master Chef, knowing that He will never leave you nor forsake you; that's His promise. He will always provide for you; that's His promise. So hold fast to that faith, to *your* faith, which is a knowledge of the *saving* faith of Christ. Hebrews 11:6 puts both types of faith in one verse: 'Without faith it is impossible to please Him: for he that comes to God must believe that He is, and that He is a rewarder of them that diligently seek Him.'

"There is one more step that I want to share with you today, and that is acceptance. Have you accepted Jesus Christ as your Lord and Savior? I didn't present this appeal to many of you when I first arrived here, for the reason that we need to have a relationship and some kind of faith in place in order to truly accept Christ. It is virtually impossible to accept something you know absolutely nothing about, and I would always caution you against it. This is one of the problems in the world today, accepting without investigating.

"No one in their right mind would accept a job offer without first knowing exactly what the position entails or if they're even qualified. Fortunately, when you enter the service of the Master Chef, He knows your qualifications better than you do. He will always find the best position to use those God given talents for His purpose, and provide on the job training to help you grow.

"I must warn you, once you accept Jesus Christ and commit to following Him, you will have an instant enemy. Satan hates God and His word, and will do anything to rip you from your Savior's arms and cast you into his own darkness. Sometimes his attacks are obvious, but more often they are very, very subtle. Satan works by degrees, slowly chipping away at the foundation of your faith, leading you to push God's word from your life little by little. He has been working nonstop in the Christian church for 2,000 years, wooing them little by little to a disregard for Biblical truth.

You can see it everywhere if you really look. You'll see entire churches completely ignorant of God's commandments, compromising God's irrefutable truth, and completely disregarding large portions of Scripture. It's these ungodly deceptions that we must guard against in order to follow our Lord and Savior.

"Revelation 18:4 calls us to 'come out of her; lest you be partakers of her sins.' That means come out of the deceived churches who are not keeping the commandments of God. Too many churches are keeping the traditions of men, sinning against God. The only way you are ever going to be able to recognize these deceptions is by reading and studying the Bible. God's Word fortifies us against the enemy's lies. There is no denying scriptural truth.

"There are many people who will tell you that all you have to do is pray a prayer accepting Christ as your Savior, and you are saved, and can go about your business, doing whatever you please, because Jesus' blood covers all your sins. The Bible can certainly seem to present this theory, if you are only reading small, specific parts of it. But there are many other scriptures showing us that true acceptance of Christ means we no longer desire sin, and we obey, not because we *have to*, but because we love Him so much that we would rather die than sin against Him! I am thrilled for anyone who accepts Christ on their deathbed, and I know that the Lord will accept every sincere plea for forgiveness and grace. There are millions of people who come to the truth at the eleventh hour, and those people will only need that one ingredient for salvation, because they have no time left to produce the fruits of sanctification. For the rest of us, however, there is much more.

"The amazing thing about following Christ is that, as our relationship with the Master Chef grows, so does our desire to serve Him and do the things that please Him. God gives us His commandments for our protection, because He loves us; because *He is good*. He knows what will make us happy, and His commandments are simply guideposts to keep us on the path of true joy. They are not a burden, but a blessing!

"I cannot let you leave here today without giving you an opportunity to begin this incredible journey of service to the Master Chef. If you desire to accept Christ as your personal Lord and Savior, please join me here in front as we sing 'Great is Thy Faithfulness.' Please, come and accept God's unending faithfulness to us."

Steve stood and began playing the hymn on his guitar as everyone rose from their seats and praised the Lord together in song. It was a wakeup call for many to hear these words from this man who was now the friend they had come to love. Even though most of them had heard several little messages from Mike, to hear him preach with such power and passion stirred their hearts and filled them with joy at their new understanding of God and His love.

Bigger and Better

A few weeks after the Ultimate Buffet was launched, Mike began extensive training with Steve, grooming him to oversee all operations of the kitchen. As Steve became more and more proficient at running things, Mike gradually pulled back. Mike needed to be free of being shift locked so he could take care of other critical issues, and Steve, a model student, absorbed knowledge and displayed proficiency beyond Mike's expectations.

Mike and Phil continued their daily walks, and it was hard to tell who enjoyed them more. The two men had formed a deep bond of mutual respect, built on the foundation of their shared faith. They both thrived on the spiritual conversations and brainstorming sessions that took place each day as they exercised in the fresh air. Phil considered this time each day to be as important to his recovery as his dietary changes.

One morning as they walked, they were stopped by a police car.

"Hi there Phil," officer Jackson greeted him. "I thought that was you. How are you doing? You know you really gave us a scare with that heart attack."

"Hey Jackson, I'm doing really well. How about you?"

"I'm great. You look like you've lost some weight too," Officer Jackson observed.

"Over 60 pounds now," Phil proudly replied. "Jackson, this is Mike, my chef and manager and…" Phil hesitated before finishing. "And my exercise trainer. Mike, this is Jackson. He's one of the leaders of the softball team that we sponsor."

"Nice to meet you Jackson," Mike said, shaking the officer's hand. "I saw your championship trophies from the last two seasons. You guys must be good."

"That's just because everyone thinks we're going to ticket them if they beat us," Jackson replied with a chuckle.

"And you probably would, too!" Phil said, as the three men laughed.

"Hey Mike," Jackson said, "you could probably get our guys in shape too. We've got some really big boys."

"I can do that," Mike said.

"We've got about a dozen games left in the season," Jackson said.

"When are your games?" Mike asked.

"We play every Tuesday and Thursday until the first week of October. Then there's a tournament, and we're done for the year."

"Tell you what," Mike said. "You give me two weeks to prepare, and I'll set up some motivational health meetings for you all to attend."

"Sounds great! Just let us know when and we'll be there. I've gotta run; great to see you, Phil. And it was nice to meet you, Mike."

"Take care, Jackson," Phil waved to his friend. "So Mike, are you really going to put together health classes for the police officers?"

"Sure, that's easy," Mike said as they resumed their walk. "I mean, look at you! People just need to be educated about healthier choices. Once they know what to do, they can begin taking steps toward a healthy lifestyle. Don't worry; I think you'll be pleasantly surprised."

Phil didn't like surprises, but he trusted Mike. "Anybody else, I would hesitate, but with you, go for it."

Mike grinned. "OK! Now, we're going to need to spend some money."

"What? We just spent thousands of dollars on the buffet."

"And we made most of that back in one day," Mike reminded him. This is an absolute necessity Phil. We need to expand."

"Expand? No way! That would cost tens of thousands of dollars, and we just don't have it. Besides, what do you need that we don't already have?" Phil asked.

"I need a bigger kitchen," Mike said.

"Ha! That's not going to happen," Phil replied confidently.

Mike grew serious. "Phil, have I ever steered you wrong? I'll get it done for less than five grand."

"Get serious, you can't do a kitchen expansion for five thousand dollars. There's no way!"

"I can. Probably less than five grand, but I'm giving myself a little cushion."

Phil couldn't see how it was possible to do a kitchen expansion for a mere five thousand dollars. But, knowing what he knew about Mike, he let his curiosity get the better of him. "Alright, he sighed. I'll bite. What do you want to do?"

"Not want to. Have to. We *have to* do this, so get on board, Captain! God will provide for all of our needs, even if it costs $30,000.00 dollars. Which it won't," he added as Phil glanced at him sternly. Seeing Phil's gaze soften, Mike continued. "We need to move the walk in cooler and the walk-in freezer outside."

Phil thought in silence for a moment, and then the lightbulb went off in his mind. "Yes! That genius! I love it! Tell me what you're thinking."

"Well, they're both really big coolers, so I'll need to place them right out the back door. We'll have to case them in because of the weather, of course. I'd also like to have a huge dry storage room out there, too. Then the kitchen is actually expanded right to the back wall and doors where the coolers will be. And with very little financial investment at all, you just got an extra almost thousand square feet of kitchen."

Phil's eyes lit up with excitement. "Do it! Whatever it takes, just do it. If you can layout the plans, I can get the county out here next week."

"Perfect. This will work, because we're really not adding anything major, just moving the existing things around. We'll have to have a few people on hand to get the coolers moved fast, in a day," Mike explained. "Steve is taking care of just about everything now, and the new menus have made the kitchen run much smoother. I'd love it if we could go down to the county this afternoon. We are so crowded in that little prep kitchen. It's killing us in there."

"Let's do it!" Phil said emphatically.

Thanks to Phil's connections at the county planning offices, the permit was issued on the spot. Inspections were not even necessary for such a simple move. After a quick stop by the health department to ensure the appropriate regulations were implemented, they were ready to begin the expansion.

Phil and Mike went over the plans for days, deciding where everything would go and how to get it done most efficiently. Phil was always calculating the framing and roofing costs, while Mike was focused on the kitchen's functionality. Mike even convinced Phil to put in another two-thousand dollars to make the expansion even bigger, and with the permit already signed off, they really had an open door to do whatever they needed.

The biggest question was whether to build the room first, then move the coolers, or move the coolers and then case them in. For the outdoor appeal, Phil won the argument to build the expansion first. It was going to be more expensive that way, but Phil knew that doing it right would pay off, especially since they were doing all of the labor themselves.

Phil worked hard, spending day and night on the framing and drywall. In the process, he decided to build the frame nearly twice the size of the original plan. Fortunately, as far as his friends at the planning office were concerned, as long as it was done right and came with a free meal, inspections were approved. Phil brought in an electrical contractor to put in the lighting and electrical outlets. Within a week, the walls and roof were up and ready for the coolers to be moved in.

The food from the freezer was transferred into the cooler, and the freezer was moved first. Once the freezer was up and running, all of the food went into the freezer while the coolers were moved. After two chaotic days of trying to function with the restaurant in disarray, the coolers were moved.

As Phil and Mike looked over the large space left over for dry storage, Phil had an idea. "I think we need to take this area here and case it in as an office for the kitchen manager, and take this area and put in a booth for the employee break room."

"Sounds great to me," Mike said. "And we'd still have room on the other wall for prep counters during busy events."

For the final touch, Phil brought in a tile guy to lay down the floor with health department approved materials, and the entire expansion was done in less than a month.

All of the employees gathered together that Sunday for a small ceremony before the doors opened for the Ultimate Buffet. Mike handed Steve a pair of scissors to cut the ribbons crossing the two huge entryways cut out of the restaurant walls to access the expansion.

Phil led the group in a prayer of dedication. "What a blessing it is to have this growth and dramatic increase of functionality. We thank you Lord for this blessing. Thank You for providing the funds and the resources. May we always use this property for Your glory. Amen."

"Amen," chorused the group.

After Steve cut the ribbon to the cheers and applause of the group, everyone dispersed to their various stations, while Mike and Phil headed out for a walk.

"Okay," Mike said. "How much?"

"How much what?" Phil asked.

"How much did it cost? I know I could have done it for under five like I promised, but you went all crazy with this bigger, better renovation. Not that I'm complaining, but really, how much was it?"

"Out the door, it was nine thousand, not counting labor. So for about ten grand, it's well worth it."

"It sure is! Can I give you a couple other things to keep in mind that we are going to need?"

By now Phil knew that every time Mike said something like that, it was going to mean sacrificing for a later reward. "OK, I'm ready. Shoot." Phil braced himself for the sticker shock.

"I'd like to get a soft-serve ice cream machine. They're about ten to fifteen thousand at the low end. We can have that in the Ultimate Buffet on Sundays and in the summer for an in-house ice cream parlor."

Phil nodded thoughtfully. "I like it," he said.

"That was easy. Should I keep going?" Mike didn't want to push Phil too hard, but he also didn't want to give up his vision. Seeing Phil's amiable grin, he continued. "We should also look at expanding the parking lot."

"Great minds think alike!" Phil chuckled. "I've been thinking the same thing. I've got 20 acres here."

"Really?" Mike was surprised.

"Oh yes. Back behind that scattered tree line is all ours too. I've wanted to put in a nice big truckers' parking lot."

"It makes sense, since we have a lot of truckers parking out in the dirt now, and there's often not enough room for customers' cars on the asphalt," Mike agreed.

"Let me work on that Mike, and I'll see if I can design a better way to park those semis. After all, those truckers have been our bread and butter since we opened this place, and I want to take care of them."

"If you really want to take care of the truckers, put in a couple shower stalls for them to use and they'll be here in droves," Mike suggested.

"Now, that's smart thinking!" Phil was getting excited at the possibilities.

"If we can expand the lot, I'd like to have a Farmers' Market out here next summer," Mike added. "We can rent out the spaces, and trade for food," Mike said. "This will create a much stronger healthy lifestyle presence in the community, and higher traffic for the restaurant."

Mike turned to Phil with a somber expression. "There's one last thing you need to do," he said. "Get a house outside of town. Ten or fifteen miles out. One with a big steel barn and some acreage. Get a generator too, with a large fuel tank, and propane tanks, more than you think you would ever need. You're going to need to stock plenty of food and supplies, too."

"Now you're scaring me a little," Phil said. "Why are you so adamant about this?"

"Because I know what's coming up in the near future, and you are going to need it. Trust me on this one Phil, just do it. God will guide you to the right property."

"I'll start looking into it. What's coming up?"

"As the Bible says, 'wars and rumors of wars,' and 'earthquakes in diverse places.' There will also be plagues and violence; suffering like nothing the world has ever seen. I don't mean to scare you, just prepare you.

"Well, this is all a little unnerving. I thought God would always provide for all our needs. Why would we need to prepare like everyone did for Y2K, which never happened?" Phil asked.

"Y2K was a manmade event, but Bible prophesy is guaranteed. It will happen. In fact, it's already started, and we are right in the middle of it. It's only going to get worse as we near the end. And God *is*providing for all your needs. He is providing you the funds to do this. You're making more money every month now than you were making in a year before. And God wants you to prepare a place of refuge for those who haven't had time or ability to prepare for themselves. This isn't just about you; this is also about what you need to do for your fellow believers. God has blessed you, so that you can bless others."

"I will do that, Mike," Phil said solemnly. "We've been wanting to get a new place anyway. Now, on another note, what are you going to do for the healthy living classes?"

Mike grinned mysteriously. "I'm not telling you anything; you'll have to see for yourself. But I will say you aren't going to want to miss it!"

Let's Get Healthy!

A few weeks later, Phil was reading the morning paper and was surprised to read the front-page headline 'Country Cafe Presents Health Series,' followed by an extensive article spotlighting the restaurant. Phil looked over his paper at Jenny, who was looking back at him with a guilty look in her eyes.

"Did you know about this?" Phil asked.

"Yes," Jenny replied hesitantly. It was clear from the look on her face that she knew more than she was saying.

"What are you two up to?" Phil asked, his curiosity growing.

"You're just going to have to wait and see," Jenny answered with a mischievous grin.

"You spent some money on this, didn't you?"

"Not a lot. And look at the exposure we're getting."

Phil continued reading the article. 'The event is free to attend, but seating is limited.'

"So it's free? We're spending money on this and we're not going to make anything back?" Phil's voice took on a tone of consternation.

Jenny smiled and gently touched his arm. "Read on."

"'6:00pm dinner for only $10.00,'" Phil read. "'Classes will be presented on Mondays and Thursdays, with opportunities to purchase healthy meals for home…' Ok, now that's good stuff. You may really have something here."

"Mike is going on the local TV station today, too." Jenny added.

"Boy I tell ya, this Mike really is something else, isn't he?" Phil chuckled.

"He sure is," Jenny said. "And he does everything with such simplicity; that's the amazing part."

"You know, he said we need to get another house."

"Really?" Jenny asked.

"Yep."

"Hmm. that's interesting. I was getting my hair done yesterday, and Maggie was there and told me that she and her husband are moving to Kentucky. They put their house up weeks ago, but haven't gotten a single offer. It's out about 10 miles past the restaurant on a 25 acre plot."

"Let me guess, it has a big pole barn, too?" Phil asked, already certain of the answer.

"Why, yes it does! How did you know?" Jenny's eyes widened in surprise.

Phil shook his head in disbelief. "The Master Chef does it again. Mike just told me last week that God would show us a house outside of town, and he described what I'm guessing is that exact property," Phil said.

"Sounds like we may be moving," Jenny said. "I would be

so happy if it all worked out!"

"Well, call them and feel out what they might take for an offer, and then get in touch with our realtor to make sure we do everything right. I'll go down to the bank and see how much we can pre-qualify for."

"Okay! I have a lot to do today, so we'd better get going. And look good tonight, because I have a felling you'll be giving a testimony."

Mike was gone all day, leaving Phil to wonder what was in store for them at the health meeting. Finally, around 3pm, Mike and Steve showed up with a van full of groceries.

"Where have you boys been?" Phil asked, looking over the grocery haul.

"Why, were there any problems?" Steve hefted a full bag onto the counter and turned to head back to the van.

"No, I just haven't seen either one of you all day." Phil stepped aside as Mike carried in a flat of produce. So, what's with all these signs going into the banquet room saying 'Phil's Not Allowed!' and 'Stay Out!'"

"You didn't look, did you?" Mike asked.

"Not a chance. Jenny's here, and she about broke my hand when I tried." Phil laughed, shaking his sore hand.

"Good! Now, can you please help us get this van unpacked? We're running late," Mike said.

In the van were what had to be hundreds of dollars' worth of food. Cases and cases of items filled every square inch of the back of the van. When they stacked up all the boxes, it seemed like enough to feed the entire town for a week.

"Phil, I need you to open all these boxes and label the food. You only have a few hours, so let's get Jenny and maybe Kimmie over here to help," Mike instructed. "Is Kimmie here yet?"

"I'm here," Kimmie said, coming out of the break room. "Just in time."

"Great. Kimmie, here is all the food that needs to be labeled and when that's done, we need to display it in the banquet room," Mike said, then added emphatically, "And don't let Phil go in there!"

"Yes, Chef!" Kimmie called over her shoulder as she hurriedly began unboxing the food.

Jenny brought the price labels over, designed with the restaurant's new logo. While she and Kimmie were labeling, Steve and Mike were racing to get food in the ovens for dinner. They scrambled in and out of the banquet room as Kimmie dashed back and forth with the labeled food, careful to keep Phil from seeing in.

"You spent a lot of money, didn't you?" Phil asked his wife.

"No, *you* did," Jenny replied, laughing.

As the dinner hour drew near, Mike, dressed in a sleek black chef's coat, called everyone together for a meeting. They all gathered in the kitchen, which now had plenty of room for everyone.

Mike began an inspiring devotional talk. "Being here in the kitchen, we know that we always need to take responsibility for our actions. If we make a mistake, we admit to our error. In the Master Chef's kingdom kitchen, when we make mistakes, we confess. Don't try hiding your mistakes. The Master Chef already knows what happened, just like in the Garden of Eden. Keep in mind, the very first confession was when Adam told God what happened in the garden. Without that first confession, who knows where we would be today.

The Master Chef loves to hear our confessions. it's not that He wants us to sin, but He loves the fact that we are willing to confess when we do. That's what makes the work environment in the kingdom's kitchen so much better. When people confess, they can move forward and learn from their mistakes. Everyone who works for the Master Chef knows what a relief it is to confess when they have done wrong. It's like a big burden being lifted off of your shoulders, to no longer hide or ignore the truth of your errors. And the truth shall set you free!"

"Okay, Okay…" Eddie interrupted. "I was the one that forgot the battered fish in the fryers. It's my fault all that fish was torched beyond recognition."

"I knew that," Mike said with a knowing smile. He continued, "We all know that the Master Chef forgives us of all our sins. He promises that what He says, He will do. What a wonderful feeling it is to be cleansed! It's like a long, hot shower after a hard day's work in a dirty environment. And it doesn't matter how dirty you get, The Master Chef can clean you up. Confession is a humbling but necessary act. Many people are so filled with pride and selfishness that they refuse to confess. They will do anything they possibly can to conceal their faults, either hiding their sin or ignoring it altogether.

"Far too often I've seen relationships ruined because someone is too stubborn to apologize. An apology is a form of confession. So many refuse to say 'I'm sorry.' Why? Because Satan has a death grip on their hearts, leading them to pride over humility. This is most damaging in families. Thousands of divorces could be prevented if only the spouses would learn to say 'I'm sorry.' Friendships are destroyed because people refuse to simply apologize. Jobs are lost and business relationships are ruined because of foolish pride. If you make a mistake, just admit it. Apologize and correct the wrong doing. A simple, heartfelt apology goes a long way. It will preserve your relationships with those you love, including the Master Chef.

"We can learn a big lesson from the Master Chef through His simple solutions to what we perceive as complicated problems. He once shared with me a way to overcome conflict with the acronym L.A.S.T. Listen, Apologize, Solve, Thank.

"The first thing you need to do is listen. Listen to the other person. What are they upset about? Second, apologize. Say you're sorry for your part in the situation, whatever it may be. Don't ruin a perfectly good apology with an excuse. Too often, people follow up an apology with an excuse, which voids out the apology altogether. People don't want to hear excuses, they just want to hear an apology. Third, solve the problem. How can you correct the problem and make it right again? Fourth, thank them for bringing the issue to your attention, and for their forgiveness and understanding.

"It's the same when we commit sins against God. He points out our error, we apologize, we solve the problem and figure out how we will keep it from happening again, and then we thank Him for His showing us our sin and extending His forgiveness, His mercy and His grace.

"1John 1:9 says 'If we confess our sins, He is faithful and just to forgive us our sins, and to cleanse us from all unrighteousness.' This is a simple approach to the concept of confession, but it works. It works in our everyday lives with family, friends, and even coworkers.

"The word confession also has another meaning, which is the same as a 'profession.' In 2 John 1:7 it says that claiming Jesus Christ is a *profession* of your faith. To profess Christ is to confess Him and lay claim to His gift of eternal salvation, but to deny Christ is to deny yourself that eternal life. Confession is one of the most important aspects of the Christian walk. The Lord loves both types of confession, as they both draw us closer to Him."

Mike bowed his head, the others joining in and pressing into a familiar huddle. "Lord," Mike prayed, "remove our thoughts and replace them with your thoughts. Give us the words that need to be spoken to a community in need of health. We offer ourselves up to You to be used for Your glory, and we thank you for the ultimate offering of sacrifice that You made for us on the cross. Please Lord, bring us those that are ready to hear Your message and speak to their hearts tonight. Thank You for your never ending love and care. In Jesus' name, Amen."

"Amen." Everyone crowded around the door, eager to enter the banquet room and see the Phil's reaction to the room.

Mike opened the doors and stepped to one side as Phil leaned in to catch his first glimpse. The Ultimate Buffet was now transformed into a marketplace of healthy foods. Everything from mouthwatering salads to nutritious entrees were ready for sale in a grab-and-go format. The entire banquet room really stood out with beautiful, oversized photos of fresh foods displayed on the walls. It was another amazing transformation.

Phil was speechless as he took it all in. The tables were set up with checkered tablecloths of green and white. Against the far wall, opposite the Ultimate Buffet, was an elevated speaking platform with a podium and two speakers connected to a new sound system.

Finally finding his voice, Phil turned to Mike and asked "How much?"

Mike grinned coyly and replied with one of Phil's classic lines. "How much what?"

"You know what. How much did all of this cost?"

"Well that's kind of hard to say at this point. It all depends how much we sell. The food went over my $5,000 budget, and all the other stuff came to about $4,000, so that's about $9,000, plus labor... Hey, that's *exactly* what you spent on the expansion," Mike's eyes gleamed merrily as he watched for Phil's reaction.

"You spent ten thousand dollars?" Phil asked, his voice edged with a combination of shock and consternation.

"Well, the dry goods are guaranteed to sell over the next few weeks, and those will generate well over $5,000 in profit, so in actuality, you got all of this for free!" Mike exclaimed.

Phil let Mike's words digest for a few seconds, then replied, "Way to go, Mike. You just earned yourself a raise!"

Everyone hurried to their assigned stations, and Mike signaled the pianist seated at an electric piano to begin playing. People began arriving at 6pm and Jenny, Mike and Phil got right to work greeting the guest and showing them to their seats. Over one hundred people arrived for the $10.00 dinner featuring the vegan meatloaf. By the 7pm, well over 175 people were packed into the banquet room with not an empty seat in the house, and even more were overflowing into the restaurant itself.

Mike stepped onto the platform, and the pianist faded out the gentle, soothing background music so he could speak.

"Welcome!" Mike boomed into the microphone, immediately drawing the attention of the crowd as the room fell silent. "I'd like to thank you all for coming. Wow! We have a packed house today! Amen!"

A couple dozen people shouted, "Amen!"

Mike smiled at the audience. "We are all here this evening for a common purpose - to get healthy!" The crowd applauded enthusiastically. "We all want to be our best, but most of us need some help getting there. This really is an upside-down world that we live in. Fast food is on every corner and manufactured junk lines the shelves of nearly every aisle of the grocery store. To illustrate just how mixed up we have become, I was in a discount store the other day and there was a framed poster that said 'Never trust a skinny chef.' But shouldn't it say 'Never trust a fat chef?'" Mike waited for the crowd's laughter to subside, then continued. "I couldn't have said that 50 pounds ago, when I used to weigh 275 pounds. So I know what some of you are going through, and I know how to help you. Does anyone want to lose a quick 20 pounds the easy way? Just wear black!" He gestured to his attire as the crowd dissolved into gales of laughter.

"But in all seriousness, excess weight comes from excess calories, excess fat, and excess sugars. One of the most prevalent health problems is excess cholesterol from saturated fats and animal fats, leading to clogged arteries. We can help you lose the weight and get healthy once and for all. Every Monday and Thursday throughout the winter, we are going to be meeting right here for lifestyle educational classes. We want to make this the healthiest city in the state!

"Tonight, you have taken the first steps on your journey to good health by joining us here at the Country Cafe. And each day in our restaurant, we work to make our food not only taste great, but be better for you. We no longer use hydrogenated oils, and we have reduced the sugar, salt, and fat in all of our menu items. Have you loved this new menu?" As the crowd cheered, Mike shouted energetically, "Then let's get healthy!" As the applause died down, Mike wiped his brow and said, "Whew... I think we just burned at least a hundred calories." This time, he joined in with the group's laughter.

"Later, I'll explain some of the unique symbols on our menu, such as fat free, gluten free, and dairy free, but first I want to introduce you to the man of the hour, Dr. Tim Foster." Mike stepped aside as Dr. Foster approached the platform.

"I'm really not the man of the hour tonight; that's Phil. Phil, come on up here." As Phil stepped up to the platform, Dr. Foster continued the introduction. "For those of you that don't know, Phil is the owner of this restaurant and six months ago, he had a heart attack. How are you feeling now, Phil?" Dr. Foster asked.

Taking the other microphone, Phil replied, "I feel great!"

"Well let's see if the results say the same thing. First things first: it's time to weigh in." Jenny carried a scale to the platform carefully checked to make sure it was at zero. "Six months ago, your weight was 392 pounds. And now?" Dr. Foster waited as Phil stepped onto the scale, then jumped off quickly and removed his shoes, coat and watch before stepping on again. Jenny checked the number and proudly shouted, "315 pounds!"

"315 pounds!" Dr. Foster projected with the mic. The crowd rose for a standing ovation as Phil and Jenny put their arms around one another and began to cry.

"That's 77 pounds lost in six months," Dr. Foster said. "That's quite a victory for this couple who didn't know six months ago if they were going to spend another day together. So, what would you like to say about your success?" Phil tried to respond to Dr. Foster's question, but the words just wouldn't come out. Phil remained speechless as he wiped his eyes and tried to regain his composure.

"That's not all, Phil," Dr. Foster continued. "Like Chef Mike said earlier, the outside appearance is not nearly as important as what is happening on the inside. I have the results from the blood test we did a few days ago. Do you all want to hear them?" A chorus of yeses answered back, but Dr. Foster grew serious and said "Sorry, but I can't do that. It would be illegal for me to reveal the test results because of confidentiality laws. Unless... it's okay with you, Phil?" Phil nodded his head in assent as the crowd cheered excitedly.

"Okay, here we go." Dr. Foster opened the envelope and paused, letting the anticipation build. Finally, he said, "At the time of your heart attack, your HDL was at 27, which is way too low. Now, it's at 43. We still need to get that number higher, and it will go up as you continue to exercise. But even better, your LDL was at 221, which is very bad. Now it's 108 - much better! Your triglycerides were 341, now they're 120. And here's the big one. Your cholesterol was at 970, and now... it's 190!" The applause was deafening.

"These results are simply remarkable. And they were achieved with no statins, no drugs other than one pill because of your heart attack, and I am taking you off of that. Congratulations, Phil. I'm so proud of you! And you too, Jenny. I know Phil couldn't have done this without your support and encouragement." Jenny smiled and squeezed Phil's hand. "Thank you, Dr. Foster. You and Mike made it happen. And by the way everyone, nearly all of Phil's meals came from this restaurant." In response to the surprised looks on everyone's faces, she said, "I don't cook a lot," and joined the crowd's laughter.

"I'm curious Phil," Dr. Foster said. "What have you been eating?"

Phil cleared his throat, tears still shining in his eyes as he reached for the microphone Jenny held out to him.

"Well, first off, thank you all so much for all of this support, and let me tell you, this journey really hasn't been nearly as difficult as I thought it would be. I've been eating like a king! Well, actually, I eat like a king for breakfast, a prince for lunch and a pauper for dinner. Mike prepares a large breakfast every morning, and that's why you'll see that our new breakfast menu has bigger portions than you might expect. As I learned from Dr. Foster, we should have the biggest meal for breakfast, a smaller lunch and an even smaller dinner. And I feel so much better today than I ever have before!"

"I think we also need to tell everyone what types of foods you're eating," Dr. Foster interjected. "Phil is on a strictly plant based diet. Without it, I don't think he would be with us today. In case you're wondering, a plant based diet, sometimes referred to as a vegan diet, is 100 percent animal free. No killing cows or chickens for your dinner. And none of the chemicals and hormones that they are injecting the animals with..."

"Whoa, Careful doc," Phil interrupted. "We're in a restaurant here!" The crowd laughed as he continued, "We still have the best burgers in town! And now we have the best veggie burgers too!"

Doctor Foster chuckled. "Got it, Phil. Anyway, a plant based lifestyle really is the healthiest one on the planet, and we are going to show you over the next hour, and in weeks ahead, some powerful and compelling facts, as well as how simple it is to make the switch to plant based foods."

"Before we continue," Phil said, "I'd like to bring my whole team up here. Come on up here, guys." The staff came up on stage, and Phil gave each of them a hug, then continued to speak. "Jenny and I don't have kids of our own; we haven't been blessed that way. But these are our kids. our whole team here are like sons and daughters to us. This is my family, who have supported me through every step of this journey, and with God in our hearts, there is nothing we can't do together. Thank you all so very much. From the bottoms of our hearts, we thank you."

Phil walked off the platform with the others, while Mike and Dr. Foster remained and presented scientific facts to support a plant based diet for almost an hour. At the end of the presentation, Mike made a few parting announcements.

"I want to remind you all that there are plenty of grab-and-go meals over on the buffet, including a full line of packaged granolas, oatmeal toppings, and healthy snacks, at great prices. We also have a scale for you to do a weigh in, and Jenny will write down your information so we can follow your progress. If you want to invite people here for Thursday's meeting, we will have a similar format, except without all the surprises and tears. So if you know anyone who couldn't make it tonight, let them know that they need to join us on Thursday. Then all next week, you can come in anytime to get your blood tests done."

"There are two types of tests you can do," Dr. Foster added. "A fasting test is the best, and to do that, you cannot eat or drink anything except water for ten hours prior to the test. Or, you can do a non-fasting test, and for that one you cannot eat for two hours prior.

"Make sure you come in next week and get tested," Mike concluded. "Thank you all so much for attending. May God direct your paths physically, mentally, and spiritually. We want you to be healthy in every way. Be blessed."

After the meeting, there were lines everywhere as the crowd eagerly snatched up the grab-and-go items, excited to try these new, healthy foods. The team restocked as fast as they could, but quickly ran out of the pre-made entrees and salads that Steve and Mike spent days making. Jenny watched in disbelief as the items flew off the tables, Lisa and Kimmie scurrying to restock as fast as they could until everything was gone. Jenny looked up from one of the tables to see Lisa asking Steve to check if there were any more items in the back they might have missed, and caught a look between the two that stirred her curiosity. It wasn't the first look of interest she'd seen them exchange, and it seemed they had found more reasons than usual to interact with one another lately. "If I didn't know better," she thought, "I'd say there is something brewing there."

After the last guest had left and the doors were locked, Steve, Mike, Phil and Jenny met in the office for a debriefing session.

"Well, How much?" Mike asked, grinning.

Steve and Phil looked up and replied in unison, "How much what?"

Even Jenny couldn't help laughing as she pulled up the totals on the computer.

"How did we do, Jenny?" Phil asked.

"Well, dinners alone were almost $2,500; only $1,400 from the banquet."

"Ouch," Mike said. That's disappointing. I thought we would do a lot more than that."

"That's the best dinner total we've ever had," Jenny consoled him. "And the kicker is, your merchandise tables brought in $1,800 for the entrees we made, and another $4,000 for the grab-and-go items. So we still grossed over $8,000 tonight.

Everyone turned to Phil for his response. He calculated in his head, then said, "How do we measure success? Only by the Lord's standards. This event was beyond any previous success we've ever had here; even more than the Ultimate Buffet's triple revenue. Financially it was a success, but more important are the lives that God will be changing through us. This health message He has given us to share will also help draw attention to His love."

"Amen," Steve said. "By the way, we ran out of the food we made in mere minutes."

"As for the grab-and-go," Phil said, looking at the numbers, "Mike, you're going to have to stock a lot more for next time. What are your projections for this?"

"I think Thursday will be just as packed, but I also think people will begin to drop off as fast as they sign up," Mike said. "More important is that we have just established this restaurant as the healthiest one in town."

"Amen!" Jenny said. "I think we need to have some lifestyle coaches, who make calls and visits and motivate and encourage those in the program."

"Yes, let's move forward on these ideas," Phil said, rising

from his chair. "Good job tonight. No, *great* job!"

The team dispersed and headed home for some well-deserved rest. As Jenny stepped out the back door in front of Steve, she noticed Lisa waiting in his car. She turned and gave Steve a questioning look. "Her car is in for repairs, so she's riding with me until it gets fixed," Steve said. "Oh, don't look at me like that, Jenny! It's no big deal."

Jenny grinned and raised an eyebrow. "Isn't it? I guess we'll see," she said with a wink, laughing as Steve blushed. "I've known you all your life, Steven, you can't put anything past me!" Steve shook his head in defeat as he headed toward the car.

"I know, Jenny, just don't make too much of this, OK?"

Jenny smiled. "I won't… yet."

Steve ducked quickly into his car, hoping the blush had faded from his cheeks as Jenny walked to her own vehicle, chuckling. In that moment, neither of them imagined that just eight months later, Phil and Jenny would be standing beside Steve and Lisa as they exchanged wedding vows and began a new life together.

Over the next few months, people showed up in huge numbers every Monday and Thursday to learn more about healthy living. The numbers didn't slip off like Mike had expected, and many people began bringing several friends and family members with them. Others came to fill their refrigerators and freezers with the delicious healthy food prepared by the staff. Sales for the restaurant increased across the board, with breakfast still a packed house every morning. Lunches and dinners increased as well. Amazingly, the more they taught about a healthy lifestyle, the busier they got. And not only were they getting busier, but all of the healthier menu options had increased in volume.

The health message was on fire!

Stormy Weather

…>>… A crack of thunder startled the group from their reverie of years past, when the health sessions were so successful in the community. Power had still not been restored after the calamity that struck just a few weeks before. The rhythmic drumming of rain on the metal roof were a relief, as the rain catchers that Mike had convinced Phil to purchase were nearly empty. Jenny and Phil got out of bed and sat at the table in the trailer, thanking God for the rain. As their prayer ended, Steve knocked on the door, accompanied by Lisa and little Mickey.

"Come on in," Jenny called out.

"It's raining in the kitchen," Steve said.

"We haven't had rain enough to notice that yet, but it's flooded in there," Lisa said.

"We have two other beds in here if we need them, but I don't think anybody's going to be sleeping, what with this weather," Phil said.

"The couch folds out into a bed and there is a full side bed in the back if we need them," Jenny added.

"Can we get the weather?" Steve asked.

"Just the national weather report, on channel 129. And the Homeland station on channel 911."

"Are you serious? Channel 911?" Lisa asked.

"Yeah, I know. Isn't that funny?" Jenny commented.

"Let's see if we can get any info," Steve said as he began searching through the stations.

The booming of thunder was coming closer and more frequent. Another knock at the door brought Joy her two children. "It's getting really bad out there!"

"I've got some reception," Steve called from the television set. "In between lightning strikes, that is. But they're just talking about the world disasters again."

Just then another knock sounded at the door and Kimmie and Edith burst into the now packed trailer. "The tornado sirens are blaring."

"Really?" Steve rushed out the door. Coming back in, he said, "Sure enough, those are the sirens. You can't hear them in here with the roof getting pounded on, but they're going off."

"So they can get electric to the sirens, but they can't get electric to the town? What's up with that?" Lisa asked.

"And they can't get the water tower pumping either?" Joy added.

"Well we should…"

"*Hey!*" Steve shouted. "Here's the weather. It's not local, but there we are right under that red zone with all the squares around it."

"Look at that map. There are red zones and squares everywhere," Jenny pointed out.

"Yeah, and look at the hurricanes, two of them," Kimmie said, pointing at the corner of the screen. "No, three!"

"I think we'd better get in the barn," Phil said, "It's the only steel frame we have."

"Yes, let's go," Jenny agreed.
The winds outside were fierce, and it was a struggle just walking the ten feet to the barn. Inside, the rest of the group were already huddled together on the beds.

"Let's get all the mattresses in the back under the loft, where there's the most protection with the double steel frame." Phil said.

The team frantically moved all the beds under the loft and sat huddled together, wondering what the night would bring. The downpour of rain drowned out the sound of the generator, making it difficult to converse. Lightning strikes were coming more frequently, leaving everyone on edge.

"Let's stay in prayer!" Steve shouted above the cacophony of noise from outside. Just then, they were startled by the crash of flying debris slamming into the side of the barn.

"Under the mattresses!" Phil shouted. "Hurry, get under them!" More debris struck, rattling the walls with a deafening roar, as though a locomotive was hurtling toward them.

There they were, twelve people scurrying for protection, when suddenly lightning struck the barn, flashing off of the steel beams, blinding everyone whose eyes were open. The ear piercing sound rendered them unable to hear anything. Blind and deaf, with the feeling of the rushing wind the only sense available to them, there was nothing left to do but pray, relying on the Lord for every breath they took. Now free from any physical distractions, they felt the peace of the Holy Spirit fall upon them, wrapping them in comfort and the realization that there truly was nothing to fear. It was actually a relief not knowing what would happen in the moments to come. Without sight or sound, their fears were eased, their peace increasing with each passing moment. All huddled together like this, they couldn't help but recall memories of Mike's huddle times…

…<<…

After the kitchen expansion, Mike's huddles were always in the prep room, where he spent most of his time, prepping as he talked. Three times a day, Mike would have a huddle to go over all of the pertinent issues of the day. And every one of them would have a theme of some sort. Everyone made it to whichever huddle they could each day, and anything of importance would be repeated at each huddle until every employee had heard the message. Often, the talks would be about Bible prophecy and things to come. Other times it would be about growing in service to the Master Chef. But every time, it was interesting and relevant, and the entire team looked forward to huddles each day.

The morning after the first health meeting, before the restaurant doors were opened, the AM team gathered together for their morning instruction. Joy and Kimmie were there with Lisa to cover the early hours in the front of the house, with brothers Eddie and Eric working the kitchen. Edith, who was now hosting, had just arrived. Mike was breading vegan chicken fried steaks for the lunch special.

"Everyone is here early today," Mike said, glancing up at the clock.

"That was a great program last night Mike," Edith said. "I think I'm going to try this healthy, plant based lifestyle."

"Me too," Lisa said. "You definitely convinced me."

"My big question from yesterday was about confession," Eric said thoughtfully. "We ask God for forgiveness, and He forgives us. I get that. But how do we forgive others? Why do we always carry this burden of remembering all the little wrongs that other people have done to us?"

"Yes, and why is it that when I apologize to someone they say 'that's OK,' but it seems as though they haven't really forgiven me? And, even when I see them again later, I get the sense that they still haven't accepted my apology?" Joy questioned.

"Well," Mike replied, "The first thing we need to understand is that the Master Chef not only forgives us of our sins, but He literally *forgets* our sins. Every one of them. Kimmie, grab my Bible on the counter there and go to 1 Kings 14:8."

Kimmie read aloud, "'And took the kingdom away from the house of David, and gave it to you: and yet you haven't been as my servant David, who kept all my commandments, and who followed me with all his heart, only to do which was right in my eyes.'"

"Remember that David had sinned greatly by having an adulterous affair with Bathsheba, and then having her husband killed in order to cover his tracks. But God refers to David as having kept all of His commandments and only doing what was right in His eyes. Why? Because God literally forgot David's sins. When we confess our sins and repent as David did, God is faithful to forgive and forget. Isaiah 43:25 says 'I, God will not remember your sins'. But we need to understand that humans, unlike God, remember what people do to them. And the second thing that is important to remember is that Christ suffers twice for all of our sins."

"Twice?" Joy asked, her brow furrowed in confusion.

"Yes. We all know that Christ died for our sins on the cross, right?" Mike asked.

"Sure," Joy said, the others nodding in agreement.

"And that the price was paid," Lisa added.

"That's right," Mike said. "But that doesn't give us a free ticket to continue sinning, just because the price was paid. In fact, every single time we sin, Christ suffers again."

"I get it," Eddie said. "And until we confess again, it's an obstacle of separation between us and God."

"It sure is," Mike agreed. "But get this: there is a big difference between forgiveness and repentance."

"Really? I thought they were basically the same thing," Eric said.

"We can all ask for forgiveness and be forgiven. But when we have true repentance, our heart is changed and we truly understand the magnitude of our sin. It's not just a knowledge that what we're doing is wrong, but a deep sorrow, accompanied by a sincere desire to change. Back in my drinking days in Las Vegas, I was drunk every day. I knew it was wrong, so I would ask God to forgive me, only to find myself back at the bottle later that same day. It wasn't until many years later that I felt genuine sorrow for all those horrible years when I was sinning against God."

"I understand," Kimmie said.

"Me too," chimed in Lisa. "And this could connect to the people who *say* they forgive you when they really don't."

"Right," Mike said. "Because they're only human, and need to feel that there is that same deep sorrow in order to truly forgive *and* forget. Without both, we are missing out on the true mending, both with God and with our fellow man."

"What an awesome Master Chef we have," Eric said. "I can really see the difference, and the need for both."

"And keep in mind that the only one who is ever going to bring up those sins of the past is Satan. He never forgets our sins, and loves to use them as weapons to make us doubt our standing with God, believing we're not good enough," Mike added.

"Oh yes," Edith said. "I have had guilt come back to me, even from things I did 40 years ago." Everyone looked in surprise at the sweet, seemingly innocent old lady, wondering what she could ever have done wrong. Edith smiled and continued, "I was a wild woman in my day. Thank God, He brought me to my senses."

"And now I see why people continue to sin too," Eric added. "Because they don't have true repentance when they ask forgiveness, which makes asking forgiveness meaningless."

"There is an age old concept that the Master Chef has continually used," Mike said. "And that is, if you make a mistake, you have to eat it. Any time we make mistakes in the kitchen and can't serve an item, 'eat it' is the common phrase. It is an understanding that your mistake cost you. Burned the steak? You eat that one. Accidentally used salt instead of sugar in the cookies? Looks like you ate that batch. When you have to 'eat' something, you never gain the profit out of it because you are consuming the cost of it, therefore you 'eat' the profit that would have been made. So the last thing we want to do is be forgiven of a specific sin and then make it again, because you can only 'eat' so many mistakes before you go belly up and are out of business."

"Well it's time to open the doors," Edith noted.

"Yes. The lunch special is vegan chicken fried steaks, and we'll have our huddle for the afternoon shift at 10:45. If you can make it, we'd love to have you," Mike said to wrap things up. "Pray throughout the day, and whenever you can, praise the Lord in song."

"He's got the whole world in His hands," Lisa sang, the others joining in. "He's got the whole world in his hands..."

The huddles continued daily, at 5:45 before opening, 10:45 before the lunch rush, and again at 2:45 for the pm shift. It was normal for people to attend two or three huddles in one day, and even if Mike was repeating half the information for oncoming employees, no one ever wanted to miss a single huddle if they could help it. Mike just had a way about him, and a manner of speaking that drew others in and captivated them. And even though Mike did most of the talking, nearly everyone participated in the conversation, asking questions and giving valuable input.

Quite often, when a question came up, Mike would wait until the next huddle to give an answer. Whenever he had an opportunity, he would look up relevant scripture and print a few as handouts. One day Eric asked, "What is sanctification?" Mike knew the answer, but wanted to get him a more complete definition, so the next day at another huddle, he went over the answer.

"Our lunch special today is this beautiful Asian salad, served with grilled garlic bread a choice of soup," Mike began.

"That just looks so awesome," Beth said. "We really should have this at the front counter for display."

"That's the best idea I've heard all day!" Mike said. "Let's get a little counter shelf right below the specials board and do that every day.

"Now, to answer the question that came up yesterday about sanctification," Mike continued. "Quite simply, it is a continual education and growing ever closer to The Master Chef. But I want to dig a little deeper, so I've got a printout for you and I'd like you to read these scriptures. Lisa, I'll let you read first."

"Okay," Lisa said. "2 Thessalonians 2:13 says 'We are bound to give thanks always to the Lord our God for you, brethren, beloved of the Lord, because God has from the beginning chosen you for salvation, through sanctification by the Spirit and belief in the truth.'"

"So we see here that salvation is linked to sanctification," Mike explained.

"Now that's really deep," Eric said. "It's almost like you can't go to heaven if you don't study."

"Well..." Mike hesitated, "We *do* have a responsibility to study scriptures, that is true. But it also means that we need the Holy Spirit to guide us, so we don't fall prey to worldly opinion and deception.

"As we study biblical truth, we develop a passion to dig even deeper and understand more. Joy, why don't you read the second scripture."

"1 Peter 1:2 says 'According to a foreknowledge of God the Father, in sanctification of the Holy Spirit, to obedience and sprinkling of the blood of Jesus Christ: Grace to you and your peace be multiplied!'"

"This really puts the whole picture together that when the Holy Spirit teaches us, we come to a knowledge of God, *and* we have a responsibility to obey to His commandments because of the blood He shed to save us."

"That's so simple!" exclaimed Lisa. "Why have I always thought of sanctification as being so complicated?"

"Because Satan complicates," Mike replied. "Our ultimate salvation really is an easy process, and sanctification *is* that process. It is an ongoing progression that should never be taken lightly, put on the back burner, so to speak. When something gets put on the back burner in the Master Chef's kitchen, people forget about it. Out of sight, out of mind. We get so busy tending to what is right in front of us that the back burner gets neglected. More things end up burned on the back burner than anywhere else in the kitchen. The Master Chef has taught us that the true purpose of the back burner is to simmer things, but we must continually go back to them to ensure that they don't simmer right into a burnt mess that can't be served. The back burner can be used for recipes that need slow cooking, or to be kept warm for a short period of time, not to be left and forgotten. Likewise, sanctification needs continual attention. Let's see, who wants to take the third passage of scripture? Eric, you got this one?"

"Sure thing, Chef. Acts 20:32 says, 'And now, my brethren, I commend you to God, and to the word of His grace, which is able to build you up, and to give you an inheritance among all them, which are sanctified.' I don't get this."

"Neither do I," Lisa chimed in. "What's the message here?"

"What it's saying here is that many are sanctified, or 'educated' in truth, but it takes more than just knowing the truth," Mike said. We need to act, and reading God's word is an action that brings a reward of grace. Let's read scripture number four. Eddie, it's all yours."

"Number four," Eddie began. "When someone is not willing to test their beliefs against scripture, it is typically because they are erroneous beliefs, which they hold in ignorance."

"Hey that's not a scripture!" Lisa interjected, eliciting laughter from the rest of the group.

"No, but I had to throw that in there because we must always be willing to test our beliefs, and learn what the Bible really says. That is part of sanctification. To me, it is also the correction of things that were not taught right the first time. Remember, we were all taught by someone else who may or may not have been teaching us biblical truth. That is why we each need to study scripture for ourselves, with the guidance of the Holy Spirit.

"Let me leave you with this," Mike continued. "There is

nothing better than managing a group of people who have been together for many years. When everyone knows one another and knows what is expected of them in their individual stations, they work together as a team and everything flows like a well-oiled machine. This team is looking out for each other, helping each other, and working toward the common goal of serving the Master Chef. The church is the same type of team, a diverse group of people all working toward a common goal. Remember, iron sharpens iron, and we need to be sharpening one another so that we can teach the Master Chef's recipes with the world. It all starts in the home, and then in our churches, at our work places, and in our communities. As we continue our sanctification process, our increasing knowledge will help us to grow in every aspect of our lives, and the Master Chef will be able to use us in mightier ways. So as we learn in this kitchen called 'Life,' let us apply these lessons to become not only well performing individuals, but also functioning members of the church. The Master Chef will soon give a final call to all people, inviting them to His great feast, and we are to be partakers in the preparations."

"Amen."

Everyone returned to their duties, contemplating Mike's words and thanking God for shining the light of understanding on their study of sanctification.

Aftermath

…>>… After the storm ended came what seemed like hours of dead silence, except for the gentle whir of the generator. Gradually, soft rays of daylight streamed through the window and awakened the exhausted group. There was a sense of comfort among them, knowing that the Lord had protected them through the night. Steve looked around and noted with thanks that the walls were still in place and everyone was unharmed.

Steve's gaze shifted to Phil, and he called out, "Phil wake up! Can you hear me?" In response to Phil's nod he asked, "Can you see me?"

"Yes," Phil replied. "I'm okay. I must have fallen asleep."

"Everybody fell asleep."

"I dreamt about the huddles that Mike used to have," Phil said.

"Me too! What a strange coincidence," Steve replied.

"How is everyone?" Phil asked.

"I don't know yet. We'd better wake them up and make sure no one was harmed."

Steve woke the others as Phil opened the garage doors. The tornado's path had spared the barn and trailer, leaving a wake of destruction over the rest of the property.

Everyone gathered outside to get some fresh air and survey the damage.

"Look at that," Eddie observed. "It was coming right toward us and then turned at the house and went right past us."

"The hand of God," Phil said, wrapping his arms around Jenny. "It was all by the hand of God."

"I'll never forget when Phil told me that Mike said we needed to buy a house outside of town with a barn, and that same week we found this place, exactly as Mike described."

"We can all thank The Master Chef for this one," Phil said. "Let's pray."

"Lord we thank You... oh, how we thank You. For the hands of protection that You have provided for us through the night, we thank You. Give us the continued confidence of knowing that Your power is far greater than any little tornado or anything else that Satan tries to throw at us. You are the Almighty God, the Creator of all things, our Master Chef, our Savior, and we *love* You. Please help us to keep our gaze firmly fixed on You so that we can continue to serve You with all our hearts. Amen."

"Amen."

"Alright, we have a lot of work to do. Let's get a group scouting the area for things we might need, resources... bodies," Phil said, his voice growing somber. "Lisa, if you could get a couple of the others and organize breakfast for everyone, that would be great. Steve, let's look at the TV reception. The generator is still running, but the wires to the barn are definitely ripped out."

"I'll get a fire going," Rick said.

"There's the satellite under the trailer," Eddie said. "I'll crawl under and pull it out.'

"Looks like it's still connected," Steve observed.

After an hour of work, everyone gathered together outside the trailer to have breakfast and listen to the news.

"I found a couple of mattresses," Kimmie said. "We could go get them after breakfast and try to create some bedroom spaces in the barn."

"That's your project for the day, Kimmie" Phil told her. "Make it happen."

The group ate quietly, their attention focused on the news reports.

"A massive earthquake *and* tornadoes? What a one-two punch. What in the world is going on here?" Kimmie asked.

"The news is really mixed this morning," Steve said. "Sure, there are reports of more devastation from around the world, but much of the talk has been on recovery and rebuilding efforts and messages of hope. Remember though, the Bible says these things will happen with increasing frequency."

"Like birthing pains," Edith added.

"And remember what Mike used to say…" Phil said, his voice trailing.

"What?" Jenny asked.

"What, what?" Phil replied.

"What did Mike use to say?" Jenny said, laughing.

"Oh," Phil chuckled. I meant that as a statement, not a question. Let's remember what Mike use to say. He said so many important things to us over the years, and it's important that we remember them. Here's a great example: what do we all remember Mike saying about prayer? He talked about the power of prayer all the time."

"Like totally, all the time," Sally said. "He used to say 'everything we do should be filtered through continual communication with our Master Chef'. I thought he was talking about himself for a while, until I realized that The Master Chef was God. Like, duh!"

"He said prayer is direct communication with God," Jenny added.

"And prayer is definitely the most powerful element we have in the kitchen," Eddie said.

"I love the way he drew a parallel between the life we live with Christ to the life we live in the food service industry," Kimmie said.

"Yeah," Sally continued. "Like you never knew what he was going to come up with next."

"Oh, I've got one for you," Steve jumped in. "Some of you were there when I asked Mike if prayer was a salvation issue, remember?"

"I remember that," Kimmie answered.

"Me too," said Edith.

"He came back the next day with a handout written up on the topic," Steve said. "Remember those handouts? It would be nice to have those right now."

"I have those sheets!" Beth said excitedly. "I've saved every one of them. I'll go get them."

Beth returned in a few moments with her Bible and a binder. She smiled as she held it up for everyone to see.

"Wow, are those all notes that Mike handed out?" Jenny asked.

"Yes they are," Beth replied. "Over a hundred of them."

"I'm telling you, I never met anyone who knew the Bible like Mike did," Lisa marveled.

"Neither did I, and I'm 77 years old," Edith said.

"He was just the most totally awesome Bible teacher," Sally said.

"Here is one on prayer," Beth said. "I'm sure there are several handouts on prayer, but this is one of the earliest ones. Let's see... I'll just read this first paragraph, OK?

"'Is prayer a salvation issue? Some people say yes, it is, while many others say it's not. We cannot be saved without a relationship with Christ, and we cannot have a relationship with Him without prayer. The Lord is not tracking every minute of prayer to see if you have invested the exact number of hours He requires in order to be worthy of salvation. Prayer is at the core of our relationship with Him. Our greatest blessing is the privilege of speaking with the Creator of the Universe! We don't have to shout across the room to talk to Him like we would an earthly companion. Our Master Chef knows every thought, sees every action. Whatever questions we have, the Master Chef hears without us speaking a single word. We can talk to Him at any time, day or night. He is there to listen to us, to reason with us. Prayer is the single most powerful ingredient we have! I urge you to put the ingredient of prayer in every single recipe you create, in every conversation, in every task, and in every aspect of your life. Prayer is our direct link to the Master Chef, and He is cares about every single aspect of your life. He is not concerned with what you can do for Him, He is deeply, genuinely concerned about *you*. The Master Chef delights to hear and answers prayer, and He is by far the best listener you will ever find."

Beth ended the paragraph and said, "I have to read this scripture he included here. 1 Peter 4:7 says, 'everything is going to soon come to an end. So be serious and be sensible enough to pray.'"

"Wow," Sally said, "That's totally for us right now. We really are in like the eleventh hour, aren't we?"

"I believe we are," Eddie said, putting an arm around her. "That's why prayer is *so* important."

"I like what he says here," Beth said, quoting some more. "'It is during times of silent, listening prayer that the Master Chef does the greatest work in our lives.
Most often, people do all the talking in their prayers and never give God an opportunity to respond. They are so busy with their lives that they come before the Master Chef to unload their requests and as soon as they're finished, it's goodbye. Now, I know that the Master Chef listens to our every petition, but we need to realize that He wants to be *involved* in our lives. He longs to be an active participant in everything we do. Give God an opportunity to respond by taking the time to listen.'"

"That's great," Jenny said. "I must have missed those

sessions. I do remember him saying that the dictionary defines the word listen as obedience."

"Oh yeah, I've heard him say that too," Joy said.

"Everyone in the kitchen has heard that line at least a dozen times," Steve said.

"He used to say that listening is a form of prayer," Lisa said. "In fact, he said it's actually the most important part of prayer!"

"So that's what kept you all in order?" Phil laughed, the others joining in. "And here I thought it was the raises I gave you."

"Ha! A lot of good that money is going to do us now," Eric replied good naturedly.

"This one is really good too," Jenny said, reading through Mikes notes. "'The power of prayer should never be underestimated. James 5:16-18 declares, "The prayer of a righteous man is powerful and effective." Elijah was a man just like us. He prayed earnestly that it would not rain, and it did not rain for three and a half years. He again prayed, and the heavens gave rain, and the earth produced its crops for the Master Chef's kitchen. God definitely listens to prayer, answers prayer, and moves in response to prayer. The power of prayer does not lie in the person praying, but rather, in the power of communion with the Master Chef.'"

"Yes!" Eddie exclaimed. "Do you really think that tornado would have just turned out of the way if we weren't all praying last night?"

"Amen!" Jenny said, "Listen to this; he quoted 1John 5:14 and said 'This is the confidence we have in approaching God, that if we ask anything according to His will, He hears us, and if we know that He hears us, whatever we ask, we know that we have what we ask of Him.' See… the key is that it's according to His will. Mike typed that in bold letters."

"And as Mike would put it," Eddie said, "It was the Master Chef's will for us to survive that storm."

"Let's all give thanks for God's will today and then go get His purposes accomplished," Phil said. "I Thank God for providing for all of our needs."

"I Thank God for protecting us and our families," Rick said.

"I Thank God for sending Mike to us," Jenny said.

"I Thank God for the family we have here right now," Lisa said.

"I Thank God for His forgiveness," Steve said.

"I Thank You God, for the words You have given us," Eddie said.

"I Thank God for the Bread of Life," Kimmie said.

"I Thank You God for loving us the way You do," Joy said.

"I Thank You God for the direction You are giving us," Eric said.

"I Thank You God for the angels that are protecting us right now from Satan's attacks," Edith said.

"I Thank God for our healthy bodies that can endure these challenges," Beth said.

"I just totally Thank You God, for everything. Amen!" Sally said.

"Amen!" Everyone echoed.

"We have a lot to do today, getting cleaned up and organized again, so let's get to it," Phil said. "We'll all meet back here when the sun goes down for dinner and fellowship. Bring your Bibles if you have one here, and we can share with those who don't. We can go over some more of the handouts that Beth has."

The group separated to begin their assigned tasks. As she walked past Phil, Jenny pulled him in for a hug and whispered "I love you!" in his ear. She had always been proud of Phil for his love, dedication and commitment both to her and to the restaurant throughout the years, but the leadership that Phil was now demonstrating filled her with deep admiration and gratitude for this wonderful man with whom God had blessed her.

Steve approached Phil, who was still grinning from ear to ear as Jenny walked away. "Hey there, lovebird, do you want to take a trip into town to see what's going on?" He teased.

"I guess we should, even though there is so much to do around here. Steve, I think I'd better leave you here in charge. You have a couple of real good workers in Rick and Eddie, so I know you'll get a lot done. Just make sure that someone is checking the news regularly today, and taking notes for the rest of us.

"OK, Steve replied. I think you should take the chainsaw," he added, "in case you need to cut down a tree in your path. I'll get the guys to gather as much wood as we can and we'll stack it till you get back."

"Great idea. We'll be back early, since we don't have to do any loading today."

Phil and Eric drove into town, stopping by the restaurant to find it in the same vandalized condition it was in when they left it the last time. As they walked through the abandoned rooms, they discovered an elderly couple sitting in the banquet room, praying.

"Are you okay?" Phil asked.

"We need food and water," the gentleman said, "but the shelter wouldn't give us anything, so we thought we would try here, but there is no food anywhere."

"What do you mean, they wouldn't give you food?" Eric asked.

"They asked if we were willing to work on Saturday, and we said we could not because we worship on Saturdays. Then they forced us out of the line."

"Just for your faith?" Phil asked. "They refused you? That's ridiculous!"

"Yes, and they were very rude and demeaning of us, too. Calling us unpatriotic, lazy and undeserving."

"I remember you two from the Sabbath morning services," Eric recalled.

"Yes. We're Andy and Florence Miller. We never missed a service," Florence said. "In fact, we were here last Sabbath and a good 70 people came. We all just sat in here together singing songs, reading a scriptures and giving thanks."

"Hop in the truck and let's go," Phil said.

When they reached the city center where the food lines were, thousands of people were standing in line or milling about. Phil walked right to the front of the line where people were being processed and sure enough, they were asking questions about faith and work abilities before distributing food. People were all getting a tagged bracelet and instructed that it was not to be removed.

They left quickly and hurried back out to the barn, where food was still plentiful. The path back was a maze of fallen trees, power lines and telephone poles, but after a couple of hours they arrived. Phil and Eric sat down with the Millers outside the trailer where Steve and a few others were watching the news. Jenny embraced Phil with a questioning glance in the direction of the newcomers.

Phil leaned down and whispered, "This couple is probably really hungry."

"I'm on it," She whispered back. Looking closely at the couple Jenny smiled warmly and said, "Welcome! You're the Millers, aren't you?"

"Why yes, we are. This is Andy and I'm Florence."

"I remember you from the restaurant," Jenny replied.

"We were there when Phil showed up," Andy said.

"Well, it's good to have you here. I'll go get another bed for you for tonight."

Jenny found Kimmie to ask if she knew where there were any more beds. Kimmie took Eric and Eddie and went off to search before the sun went down.

Jenny returned with two heaping plates of warm, hearty food for the hungry couple.

"Florence said that there were around 70 people at the restaurant last Sabbath for prayer and worship," Phil said.

"There have been more and more coming there every Sabbath. It has become the Sabbath headquarters for the community," Andy added.

"Really? That's more than we have ever seen there," Jenny replied. "We've all been up here and had no idea."

"Some of the people were saying that the rapture happened and you were all taken to heaven," Andy said.

"Those were the ones who didn't study their bibles," Jenny said matter-of-factly.

"That's right," Steve said. "There is no such thing as a secret rapture. That's a false doctrine derived from a single misinterpreted scripture. There are many scriptures that prove there is no secret rapture."
"Well, I know that, and you know that, but there are a lot of people out there that don't know scripture," Andy said. "But since none of you showed up, those with a wrong understanding of God's word were coming to their own conclusions."

"We need to be there this Sabbath," Jenny said.

"Definitely," Phil agreed. "Today is Wednesday; let's keep an eye on the news and pray for God's guidance as to what we should do."

"We still have a couple of hours before the sun goes down," Steve said. "You look exhausted. Why don't you go clean up a bit? We have full water reserves. Then you can get some rest."

Phil consented and Jenny brought some warm water from the huge cooking pot into the trailer and poured it in the sink for Phil to freshen up. Afterward, he climbed into bed for a much needed nap.

As everyone gathered together for dinner, Phil emerged from the trailer feeling refreshed and rested.

"I feel like a new man. Amazing what a good shave and a little sleep can do. I've got razors for everyone else, too. In fact, if there is anything that you really need, we have boxes of supplies up in the loft of the barn."

"The only thing we have is the clothes on our backs," Andy said.

"And we aren't even going to need those pretty soon!" Florence added.

"That's right," Andy beamed, "We're going to get brand new white robes!"

"Amen!"

"Everyone," Phil said, "in case you haven't met them yet, this is Florence and Andy. They'll be staying with us from now on, so take a moment to introduce yourselves when you can."

"Wow, what a meal we have here!" Phil exclaimed, surveying the bounty set out on the eight foot table. There was more than enough to feed the group of 14 people.

"It looks like all the fresh fruits and vegetables are gone

and we are on to the frozen foods. Let's have the blessing, then we can discuss what is going on. I would also like to finish up tonight with what Beth has on prayer from Mike's notes. Steve, can you offer prayer for us?"

"Heavenly Father we thank You for this day, and we thank You so much for enabling us to get things accomplished today. We especially thank You for the divine appointment of encountering Andy and Florence and bringing them here. Please bless us all, and forgive us our shortcomings. Thank you for this food, please bless it and the hands that prepared it to keep us nourished. In Christ's name, Amen."

"Amen."

Kimmie and Lisa did a wonderful job of thawing the frozen foods between double stacked sheet pans. It took the greater part of the day, but turned out perfect.

Phil whispered to Steve, "How's the food supply holding up?"

"We have a couple weeks' worth at the very most," he replied. "Have you heard all the gun shots?"

"I sure have, and they're getting closer by the day," Phil said, concern in his voice.

"There are a couple of possibilities," Steve said. "One is that they're hunting food and have to go farther out of town to find game. Another is that they're killing people to take what they can from them."

"Or the probable answer: both," Phil whispered. "We need to be ready. They're miles away now, but will be here soon enough."

"We have plenty of weapons and ammo," Steve said.

"No violence," Phil cautioned. "We need to arm ourselves with prayer."

After some pleasant conversation and good food, Phil turned the discussion to current events.

"Well Steve," Phil asked, "what new developments took place in the world today?

"Israel was bombed today."

Everyone looked up in shocked silence.

"Well, that's nothing new," Phil said casually.

"No Phil," Steve replied. "They got bombed right off the map."

"What? Really? What are the news reports saying?" Phil could hardly believe what he was hearing.

"They say that when the Armed Forces of the UN and US troops arrived, there was nothing left to save. The entire country is in ruin."

"This is prophesy being fulfilled," Florence said.

"Yes, and they are blaming the Muslims, naturally," Rick said.

"Well the Muslims did it, right?" Eric asked.

"A radical Muslim group, not Muslims in general. There are well-funded terrorists doing the bombing, not the people themselves," Steve said.

"All the radical Muslim movements, regardless of the name they go by, are very well-funded."

"I have a question," Beth said. "All these names we've heard over the years like Al-Qaeda, Hamas, Taliban, ISIS… they are all Muslim groups, aren't they?"
"Yes, they are," Phil said.

"And they always have a lot of money supporting their movements, don't they?" Beth asked.

"That they do," Steve said.

"Then where is the money coming from?" Beth asked. "Follow the money."

Rick had an answer they weren't expecting. "We are funding them."

"I'm totally lost on this one," Sally lamented.

"Think about it," Rick said. "All of the money for their terrorist acts comes from wealthy, powerful people and even governments. And all that wealth comes from oil, of which we are the number one consumer."

"Makes total sense to me," Jenny concluded. "If you take away their multi-billion dollar oil source, they would be over there fighting with sticks and stones."

"Extremely good point," Steve said, "It's like we're the fuel for their fire."

"I know that most Muslims are really good people," Beth said. "They are kind, loving people desiring peace and prosperity for their families."

"And I distinctly remember Mike saying that the Muslims were going to be used as a pawn for Satan to go after the true Christians, the ones who keep the commandments of God," Terri recalled.

"Yes, he told me that too," Beth said.

"Let me predict what's going to happen next," Phil said. "People of all faiths are going to put their differences aside and band together to go after the Muslim extremists."

"Just the way Mike said it would happen!" Beth exclaimed.

"And not just all faiths," Steve said. "Political sides, too. Democrats, Republicans, and Libertarians, liberals and conservatives. They will gather together for a common cause, to rid the planet of all these terrorists and anything else that they deem evil."

"But how is it determined what is or isn't evil?" Beth asked.

"Anyone or anything that does not fit their collective agenda can be classified as evil," Steve replied. It has nothing to do with what the Bible says, but about what helps or hinders their plans. Satan works through worldly leaders all the time to achieve his ends. He used the religious and political systems of the day against Jesus, against the Christians in Rome, against believers in the Dark Ages, and has continued to do so to this day. He's like a one-trick pony that never changes."

"That is so true," Lisa said. "That's exactly what Satan has been doing for generations."

"It really is a master deception being orchestrated right before our eyes," Florence added.

"Mike once told me a little story on one of our walks that I had forgotten until now," Phil recalled. "He said that in Jesus' time there were two parties that hated each other, but joined together to persecute Christ and his followers."

"That would be the Pharisees and Sadducees," Andy said.

"Yes. And in the end days, once again two opposing sides would unite to go after Christ's true followers."

"Looks like that is exactly what is happening," Beth mused.

"This is like so amazing, to see Bible prophecy totally being revealed right before our eyes," Sally said.

"The problem is that most people, even most Christians, don't know the Bible, and they don't truly know Christ," Steve said. "They only know the counterfeit; an acceptable replacement for Christ that compromises, allowing people to continue in their sinful lifestyle and calling it 'grace.'"

"Just watch!" Phil said, "They are going to come together, put their differences aside and go after God's people with a vengeance."

"And all in the name of peace," Lisa said.

"They would obtain a false peace among men by waging war against God," Kimmie said, shaking her head.

"That's the dragon slayer!" Edith shouted. "The false Christians and the non-Christians are the two sides, remember? The dragon slayer?"

The others nodded, remembering something that Mike had talked about many times before.

"Mike said that the dragon slayer would be created by false Christianity uniting with the government and even with many Muslims to fight the common enemy."

"Do you remember what he said next?" Eric asked. "I do. He said the dragon slayer would soon become the dragon and go after everyone who does not submit to his authority."

"He told me that the false Christians were the ones that we were going to have to watch out for," Steve said. "At the time, I thought that was kind of ridiculous. It seemed like such a stretch, but sure enough here it is, happening exactly the way he said it would. There was a scripture he quoted too, saying that they would kill God's commandment keeping people, and that they would be doing it in the name of God, thinking they were serving Him."

"I know that scripture," Joy said, flipping through pages. "Let me find it in the Bible."

"For the life of me, I just couldn't understand how he was so well informed, but it was all right here in the Bible," Phil said.

"He taught straight from the scriptures every time," Edith remembered.

"And now we see those scriptures coming to life," Beth added.

"Here it is!" Joy said. "John 16:2, 'You will be thrown out of synagogues. Certainly, the time is coming when people who murder you will think that they are doing the service of

God.'"

"Amazing; simply amazing!" Rick said. "Who would have thought that so-called Christians would end up becoming the enemy? I mean when Joy first told me about this I thought it was impossible, but now, it couldn't be closer to the truth."

"If possible, Satan would deceive the very elect," Andy said.

"Oh, by the way," Phil said, "People are now required to be tagged in order to get food."

"What? How in the world are they doing that?" Jenny asked.

"Everyone is asked what faith they are and what days they're willing to work. If people answer correctly, they get outfitted with a wristband and instructed not to remove it. Only then are they allowed to get food."

"I saw those on TV earlier," Rick said. "They are computer tracked, and rumor has it that if you take them off, they explode. And many people already have the computer chip implants from the healthcare laws."

"Mike said that God's people would not be able to buy or sell," Eric stated.

Edith reached for her weathered Bible and began to read. "Revelation 13:17 says 'No one could buy or sell anything without that mark, which was either the name of the beast or the number representing him.'"

"People become slaves to the world leaders without even realizing it," Florence said.

"They likely wouldn't care if they did know," Beth said. "They're too concerned with maintaining their ungodly lifestyles."

Terry, typically the silent listener of the bunch, couldn't help but speak up. "What we need to understand is that most of these people don't think they *are* living an ungodly lifestyle. Satan has slowly turned the culture upside-down to the point that people have no idea what true godliness even is."

"Yes, we live in a world where anything goes, and all sorts of sinful things are considered perfectly acceptable, even though the Bible makes it clear that those things are forbidden by God," Beth said.

"God's commandments are now considered outdated and oppressive, which has resulted in the moral decline of society," Phil said.

"People completely ignore the fact that God says in His word that He never changes and His commandments will never change," Eric said.

"Mike used to say, 'The better the lie is presented, the more absurd the truth is going to sound,'" Steve said. "And that's exactly where we are in the world today."

"Satan has really turned the world upside down, hasn't he?" Rick asked.

"He sure has," Steve agreed. "And almost no one even realizes what he's done."

"So Satan's final move is to go after the few remaining people who are keeping God's commandments," Joy said.

"Particularly the fourth one," Florence said. "Satan despises the Sabbath commandment because it is a memorial to God's creative power. God is the only being in all the universe with the ability to create. Got is creation; without Him, nothing and no one would exist. This sets Him apart as the one true God, and Satan knows that he will never be able to create, only destroy. It marks him as a false God, and that fills Him with fury."

"That's why keeping the Sabbath is becoming such a major issue," Eric said. "It is a true test of allegiance - will we serve the one true God of creation, or the counterfeit? Most of the world will be completely deceived."

"I remember Mike saying that it would first be presented through the power of persuasion, then change into persuasion by power," Kimmie said.

"And that's where we are right now," Phil said.

"You can see the progression from persuasion to power throughout history," Steve said. "First, Satan takes hundreds of years persuading men to change the Sabbath from Saturday to Sunday, even going so far as to murder anyone who didn't obey the church's order. Still, a faithful few remained true to God and His commandments. Then, he tried to convince people to do the 'right' thing for the sake of unity, saying it would please God. As a result, Sunday laws sprang up everywhere. And now the last-ditch effort is to persecute and eventually try to kill those who insist on keeping God's law."

"But anyone without a real knowledge of the Bible can't see this," Rick said.

"How can you not see Satan's massive effort to quash the Sabbath?" Lisa asked. "Anyone who obeys God's commandments is not allowed to buy or sell? What happened to freedom of religion?"

"We're way past freedom now," Phil said. "We need people watching this TV as often as possible, as long as the generator is holding up."

"But we must always pray for discernment," Steve added. "Every broadcast is designed to feed into the agenda. We have to keep aware that it's the enemy's station."

"The reality is that if you didn't know the Bible and understand its truth like we do, you would be absolutely buy into the lies hook, line and sinker," Joy added.

"'God will send them strong delusions that they should believe the lie,'" Edith quoted. "That's in 2 Thessalonians."

"It all comes back to a relationship with God," Lisa said. "As Mike always put it, 'read more, pray more and study more.'"

"Let me read you something else Mike said about prayer," Jenny added. "'When we pray passionately and purposefully, according to His will, the Master Chef responds powerfully! The secret recipe for answered prayer lies in the sincerity of the prayer. Answered prayer is not based on the eloquence of our speech. We don't have to use any special words or phrases to get the Lord's attention. In the Bible, Jesus rebukes those who pray using vain repetitions. Prayer is communicating with the Master Chef. All you have to do is come to Him with a sincere heart and He will listen. Ask for His help and He will calm the boiling pot to a simmer, the overwhelming tasks of the frantic kitchen will become manageable. The work will be done with ease and you will find peace. There is power in prayer!

"'The Master Chef's help is available for every circumstance. Philippians 4:6-7 says, 'Do not be anxious about anything, but in everything, by prayer and petition, with thanksgiving, present your requests to God. And then the peace of God, which transcends to all understanding, will guard your hearts and your minds in Christ Jesus.' You see, the Master Chef deeply desires to be intimately involved in every aspect of your life.'"

"Oh, that is so true," Beth said. "I truly never knew what 'wonderful' really was, until Christ was involved in every part of my life!"

Jenny continued, "'Chew on this: Christ says that His children will know His voice. But how will you ever know His voice if you are never listening to Him? How will you know His voice if you are constantly the one doing all the talking?'"

"Oh, that's a good one," Edith said.

Here's another one," Jenny said. "'The purpose of prayer is not merely to get answers; prayer *is* the answer!'"

"Since it's getting late, I suggest we have prayer and call it a night," Phil interjected.

Everyone bowed their heads as Phil prayed. "Father God and Master Chef, we thank You for entering our lives, and being willing to work with such flawed servants as ourselves. Your love is beyond our understanding, Your compassion more than we deserve. Lord, we are here to plead with You to change our hearts and transform us into the people You need us to be in these final days. Send Your Holy Spirit to renew our minds that we may better serve You. Oh Lord, refine our desires, that they would reflect Your perfect will. We thank You for the mercy and grace that You bestow upon us. In Christ's holy name we pray, Amen."

The Loud Cry

As Phil opened the door to the brisk morning air, Steve awoke from his spot on the lounge chair where he fell asleep last night. Joy and Kimmie had a large pot of oatmeal cooking in the crackling fire pit.

"Well good morning, sleepy head," Phil said, stretching his arms overhead as far as possible in the trailer. "Did you stay up half the night?"

"Not quite, but close," Steve replied, yawning. "It's just one thing after another in the news. More earthquakes, Australia just got hit with the worst typhoon ever recorded, and several massive volcanoes erupted somewhere in China, wiping out entire villages."

Joy and Kimmie brought cups of hot coffee for the men and sat down to join them.

"Thank you, ladies," Phil said. "You girls are up early."

"The earthquakes woke us up," Kimmie replied.

"We had earthquakes?" Phil asked incredulously."

"I didn't feel a thing," Steve said.

"You men will sleep through anything," Joy chuckled.

"What's the Pope talking about there?" Kimmie asked, pointing at the muted TV.

Steve grabbed the remote and turned up the volume.

"This is Diane Sadler reporting live from the Vatican, where the Pope is urgently calling for people around the world to honor Sunday as a day of rest. The Holy Father contends that the recent worldwide catastrophes are a result of the sin of ignoring God's holy day. In response, both the White House and the United Nations have declared that all non-emergency businesses are to close on Sundays for what they call 're-stabilization purposes.'"

"The required orders are being strongly debated on all sides, with the Federal Reserve claiming the move will restore balance to the financial markets, and Christians around the world agreeing with the Pope for reasons of faith. Some radical religious groups claim the edict is a violation of religious freedom, but for now, all businesses are required to close on Sundays."

"Wow... Did you all get that?" Steve asked. "Exactly the way Mike said it would happen."

"I wasn't sure I believed it then, but I sure do now," Joy said.

"I also remember him saying the Sunday laws would be a global requirement, and that there would be a 'loud cry,' whatever that is," Kimmie added.

"I remember him talking about that," Steve said. "That's the time when the whole world hears the truths about the Sabbath. It will be man's last opportunity to honor God by obeying His commandments before the door of probation closes.

"He also said there would be plagues, and diseases," Kimmie remembered.

"But if I remember correctly, he also said that the bride of

Christ would not receive those plagues, because once probation closes, the enemy no longer has any access to the people of God," Steve recalled.

"What is this about the close of probation? I didn't catch that," Eddie asked, joining the group.

"It's like what happened with the flood and Noah's ark," Steve explained. "Noah preached for 120 years about the coming flood, extending an invitation to come into the ark and be saved, but once he and his family went inside and the door was closed, it was too late to come in and all those outside the ark were doomed. Everyone has a choice now, but once probation closes, there are no more chances to repent."

"He quoted the scripture that says 'he who is holy let him be holy still, and he who is filthy let him be filthy still,'" Phil added.

"He also said that God would direct our paths," Steve said.

"And I remember him saying that Sabbath keepers would be regarded as terrorists and an evil that must be eradicated," Phil recalled.

"That's us! Kimmie exclaimed. We're all Sabbath keepers; does that mean they're going to be hunting us down? Killing us because we serve the Lord?"

"We are in for a lot of difficulty, but our God will bring us through it all," Joy said encouragingly.

"Let's all keep in prayer morning, noon and night, and stay focused on the Lord," Phil said.

As the others awoke to the scent of cinnamon oatmeal,

Phil read through some of the pages of Mike's classes. Once everyone had finished eating, Phil spoke to the group.

"I want to share with you one of the last lessons that Mike taught. I've been reading through the notes Joy has here and it's remarkable how they're exactly what we need in these last days. Can someone look up Ephesians 6:10-20 while I read, please? Mike wrote 'The Master Chef has given us all the ingredients we need and He is also providing all the tools necessary to overcome any obstacles that Satan places in our path. It's when we use all the ingredients and all the tools that we can receive all the power God is generously offering. The blender needs ingredients - it is useless until there is something in it to blend. The same thing is true in our Christian life. We need the tools, we need the ingredients, and we need the Master Chef to teach us the proper way to use the gifts He has given us.' Okay, who has Ephesians 6:10-20?"

"I do," Sally said. "Finally, my brothers and sisters, be strong in the Lord and in the power of His might. Put on the whole armor of God, that you may be able to stand against the wiles of the devil. For we do not wrestle against flesh and blood, but against principalities, and against powers, and against the rulers of the darkness of this age, against spiritual *hosts* of wickedness in the heavenly *places*. Therefore, we must take up the whole armor of God, that you may be able to withstand in the evil day, and having done all to stand. Stand therefore, having girded your waist with truth, having put on the breastplate of righteousness, and having shod your feet with the preparation of the gospel of peace; and above all, taking the shield of faith with which you will be able to quench all the fiery darts of the wicked one. And take the helmet of salvation, and the sword of the Spirit, which is the word of God; pray always with all prayer and supplication in the Spirit, be watchful to this end with all perseverance and supplication for all the saints; and for me, that utterance may be given to me, that I may open my mouth boldly to make known the mystery of the gospel, for which I am an ambassador in chains; that in it I may speak boldly, as I ought to speak."

"Well read, Sally!" Phil continued, "Now who knows the tools that the Bible talks about?

"The belt of truth is one," Steve said. "Mike referred to it as the apron."

"Right. Let's see what Mike says about the belt of truth. 'In Roman times, the belt held a lot of weapons and it was necessary for this belt to be fastened securely in order for the tools not to move out of place and create imbalance. In the biblical sense, the truth of the Master Chef's Word is the foundation that can keep us from being out of balance. It is the core of everything. Just as today's good professional aprons are designed to be fire resistant, God's word keeps us from getting burned by Satan's attacks. We must have on the belt of the Master Chef's truth to protect us.'"

"OK, what's another tool?"

"The breastplate," Eric said. "Mike compared it to a chef's coat. I'll never forget when he gave me my coat and brought me out of the dish room."

"Yes, the breastplate of righteousness. Good one, Eric." Phil began to read again from Mike's notes. "'It's all about the truth, and the knowledge of the truth. The righteousness that we possess cannot come from us, it can only come from the Master Chef. Anything else is false righteousness, rooted in works. There are millions of so-called righteous people out there that do not have Christ's righteousness, but their own, which the Bible says is "as filthy rags." True righteousness comes from the Master Chef, and His righteousness covers us, like a breastplate - the chef's coat, that protects our hearts.'"

"I always loved how Mike would compare biblical terms with everyday life," Kimmie said.

"There is also the chef's hat," Eddie said.

"Yes, the helmet of salvation," Phil said. "Here's what we have on that. 'The helmet is vitally important. It represents our intelligence, will and decision making. Without the head, the body cannot function. Without the helmet of salvation, we are left to follow impulse and feeling rather than refined, rational thought. We cannot save ourselves. Although we are instructed to work out our own salvation "with fear and trembling," the Master Chef is the One through whom that salvation is found.'"

"'Our mind is the most important tool we have, and the Master Chef wants us to be of sound mind and make good decisions. By putting on the Master Chef's helmet of salvation, His continual guiding presence in our minds will keep us constantly on guard. We need to be alert to keep the enemy from infiltrating our thoughts.

"'We should not allow our minds to be clouded by anything that will alter our decisions or judgements, or sway our convictions. We are constantly bombarded by so many things designed to distract our thoughts and prevent our minds from functioning properly.

"'Sometimes, our hats define us. If you see someone in a fireman's helmet, you know exactly who that person is. A hat can tell others who you are and what or whom you represent. The roman soldier's helmets were often made of beautiful engraved brass, and were a symbol of who they represented. They were heavy, too. There was no way a soldier wearing one of those helmets could ever forget who they were representing.

"'The helmet of salvation is not only a protection, but a proclamation. We are representatives of the Master Chef, the God of all the Universe. Oh what a privilege that is!

"'The Roman soldiers' helmets protected the entire head - eyes, ears and mouth included. The helmet came down over the ears, the eyes were shielded and had a small viewing area, and the helmet came around the front of the mouth. This is an important parallel to the helmet of salvation. Be careful what you hear, what you place before your eyes, what you put into your mouth and what you allow to come out of it. What you eat greatly impacts your mind. Satan wants our bodies to control our minds, but God has designed our minds to control our bodies.'"

"That's really interesting," Beth said.

"It sure is. There are more purposes for the helmet than people would think," Rick agreed.

"Anyone have another part of the whole armor of God?" Phil asked.

"There is the knife," Rick said.

"And the shield," Joy added.

"Okay, I've got what he says about the knife - which is the Sword of the Spirit - right here," Phil said.

"'The Word of God is the most powerful weapon we have. After all, Christ *is* the Word made flesh. The sword is the only tool designed for attack rather than defense. We have a lot of tools in the kitchen, but our knives are the most important implement the Master Chef has given us. In war, it is conquer, surrender or die. It is the same in our spiritual battle. It's no wonder that the Master Chef instructs us to keep our knives sharpened at all times. We sharpen our swords by spending time daily in the Word of God, and being prepared to answer temptation with a firm "it is written," just as Christ did when confronted by Satan.'"

"Did you ever see Mike's knives?" Steve asked. "Man, talk about sharp! You could shave with those knives, they were so sharp."

"Just as sharp as his spiritual sword," Edith said.

"Okay, next we have the shield of faith," Phil said, then continued reading.

"'The shield of faith protects us from the attack of the enemy. Salvation comes by faith, and through the strengthening of our faith, we have an impenetrable shield that will resist even the strongest assaults. The strength of our shield is directly proportionate to the strength of our faith. God is our shield - our Protector and Defender, and the more we believe and trust in Him, the more He is able to shield us from the adversary.

"'We are told to take up our shield *"above all."* This is because without faith, we can do nothing. All of the other armor is useless without a saving faith in Christ. Even the best armor is vulnerable without a shield to block the "fiery darts" of the enemy. Our faith prevents many attacks from ever reaching us, allowing us to move forward uninjured. In the kitchen, our trust in the Master Chef and His ability to lead shields us from conflict and confusion. The Master Chef has already planned for and dealt with so many potential mishaps, so we never have to think about them. He already has it covered. We can put our complete, unwavering trust in the One who knows what is best for us, and rest in His protection.'"

"Anyone remember what's next?" Phil asked the group. After a few moments of silence, Phil smiled and proclaimed, "The shoes! We're commanded to have our feet 'shod with the preparation of the gospel of peace.' Mike has some really great thoughts on this."

"'In the kitchen, proper footwear is vital. We need traction to keep us from slipping and thick, supportive soles so that we can stand for long periods of time without pain. In our spiritual life, the shoes of the gospel of peace enable us to step freely and without fear while we give our full attention to the battle at hand. The good news of the gospel brings peace, and that peace allows us to stand firm, whatever comes against us. And when we are on solid footing, we are able to help secure others. We are called to proclaim the good news of salvation to all the world. Having on the shoes provided by the Lord, we are ready to move, to spread the gospel of peace to everyone. Romans 10:15 says, "And how shall they preach if they have not been sent? As it is written, how beautiful are the feet of those that announce the gospel of peace, of those that announce the gospel of that which is good!" Those shoes make our feet - our witness to the world - beautiful in God's sight!'"

"What a great lesson for us in these last days," Andy said.

"We really need to keep these things in mind in the midst of all our challenges," Lisa added.

"There is one more essential component in our battle that I bet none of you can guess," Phil said.

"We've already listed all six pieces of armor; like what else could there be?" Sally asked.

"Prayer," Phil replied. "Listen."

"'Prayer is a vital part in taking up the whole armor of God. None of the tools are really doing much good without continual, earnest supplication.

"'Communication in a kitchen is absolutely crucial. Without proper communication, everything falls apart. We must communicate our thoughts, observations and needs to our Master Chef, and listen as He communicates His expectations and feedback to us. Spiritually, we can do everything we think is right, but without prayer, we really have no way of knowing if we are centered in God's will. It is impossible to have a genuine relationship with someone you never speak to. If we fail to communicate with the Master Chef, we cannot build the trust necessary for a smooth running kitchen. And if we neglect to communicate with Christ, our trust in Him cannot be developed either. The Master Chef wants to help us in any way possible - we just need to ask Him! Reading the scriptures is important, but that is only one-way communication from God to us. Our response to Him creates a dialogue, from which our relationship grows. There is simply *no substitution* for prayer.'"

"AMEN!" Steve exclaimed.

"There truly is power in prayer," Jenny said. "That's why we're all here, and that's why Phil is still with us. We prayed for God to send us the help we needed."

"Amen," Phil said. "Let's take that into consideration as we —"

Before Phil could say another word, the earth began to shake. Bigger than the tremors of the morning, trees and telephone poles swayed threateningly as the group watched in stunned silence. Thirty seconds later, the earth was still.

"I forgot what I was going to say," Phil whispered into the silence.

"Let's pray," Steve said. "Our Father in heaven, the one true God, who is beyond the clouds but not beyond our reach, we come to You in gratitude for Your faithful protection and care. Please Lord, give us this day, our daily bread, which is Jesus Christ, the bread of life. We plead for You to fill us with more and more of Your Blessed Spirit. As we prepare for Your holy Sabbath day, we pray that You will safely bring to the restaurant tomorrow those that need to be there, and keep Satan and his hosts at bay. Increase our faith and let us rejoice in this day that The Lord has made. Amen."

"Amen."

Later that day, as Steve flipped through the television channels, he discovered more sobering news. Global economic collapses were occurring and the world seemed to be coming to a standstill. Tragedies were increasing and war was breaking out all over the world. Steve caught Phil's eye and subtly signaled him to come over.

"I found another station that flickers in and out sporadically, but one thing I heard clearly is that there is trouble with 'dissenters' rebelling against the requirement to keep Sunday as a day of rest. They referred to 'stubborn radicals including observant Jews, Seventh-day Adventists and other Sabbath keeping fanatics.' They briefly showed part of an interview with a couple of pastors, showing beyond a shadow of a doubt that Saturday is the Sabbath, but they were cut off as soon as it became apparent that they were speaking irrefutable biblical truth. The reporter was scrambling to change the subject and bring the focus back to the men's disregard for law and order. He seemed desperate to quash the pastors' influence and prevent anyone else from believing what they said."

"Sounds like the 'Loud Cry' is taking place," Phil said. "They are seeking to force people to disobey God, while claiming to act in the name of God."

"These people have never had a true relationship with God, or they would know better than to follow the false teachings of men," Steve said. "Apparently, thousands of people are flocking to Sabbath keeping churches all over the world, asking to study what the Bible really says. It's amazing how the Holy Spirit is leading sincere seekers of truth. Even the mainstream media is picking up on this, because it's too big to hide, but of course, they're putting a negative spin on it. A real spiritual war has begun."

"I have a feeling we're going to have a bigger crowd at the restaurant this Sabbath than we previously expected," Phil said.

"It would be great if we could print some Bible study guides based on Mike's outlines," Steve said.

"We have a printer in the trailer; why don't you put something together," Phil replied.

"OK. I'll go through Joy's stack of Mike's writings and see what I can come up with."

"Make it a simple message," Phil said. "All about the gospel, the love of Christ, the necessity of keeping His commandments, and the Sabbath being a perpetual covenant."

"I'll get right on it," Steve said.

"I'll get a large bag of oatmeal and some other foodstuffs to feed anyone that shows up hungry," Phil added. "Our food supply won't last much longer, but we have to share it with others in need."

"Good idea. We'll also need plastic spoons and bowls," Steve suggested. "And a portable burner with butane."

That evening, everyone gathered for dinner and welcomed the Sabbath with songs of praise. In spite of the turmoil in the world around them, they were all filled with a deep, abiding peace.

"Steve put together some Bible studies for us to distribute to those who come to the restaurant tomorrow," Phil said, "and I've gathered food and other provisions. There will likely be many people at the restaurant tomorrow in need of nourishment, spiritual encouragement and guidance. We only have enough fuel for two vehicles with room for seven people, so some of you will have to stay behind. You may be better off here anyway; it could be quite dangerous out there."

"I'll go," Eric and Eddie said in unison.

"As you all know, the Pope has declared Sunday to be the official day of rest and the world governments are complying. Sabbath keepers around the globe have been declaring the truth of God's true Sabbath. Steve has been watching news coverage of the unfolding events."

"The military has been called in to shut down Sabbath-keeping churches," Steve said. Those refusing to observe Sunday are regarded as terrorists. The Pope says we must be eradicated in order to appease God, and the whole world is buying it."

"And all under the guise of unity," Rick added. "Coming together and putting aside religious differences for the good of mankind."

"Unity that can only be achieved by force is no unity at all," Beth observed.

As the group watched the evening news before bed, everyone was deeply convicted that last-day events were unfolding in front of them, just as Mike had described. A ripple of excited anticipation ran through the group as they contemplated the glorious day of redemption that was so near.

They arrived at the restaurant the next morning to find a group of around ten people waiting inside. Steve was relieved to find running water at the faucet and got to work making a large pot of oatmeal.

Steve was kept busy preparing batch after batch of oatmeal as more and more people streamed in. Everyone was given the Bible studies that Steve had prepared and invited to enjoy a bowl of hot oatmeal with raisins and maple syrup. After everyone's hunger had been abated, they all sang songs, and fellowshipped throughout the morning, the group growing larger by the hour. By noon, there were well over 200 people packed into the banquet room and spilling out into the main dining room.

Phil stepped onto the platform and raised both hands in the air as he called out to get everyone's attention.

"Good morning! What a blessing it is to worship our God on His holy Sabbath day, which He ordained and sanctified at creation."

"Amen," a number people responded enthusiastically.

"We need to understand one thing," Phil continued. "If you love God, you *will* keep His commandments."

Several heads around the room nodded in agreement.

"And that includes the fourth commandment, which reminds us of God's perpetual covenant with us. Satan has orchestrated a diabolical plan to rob us of the gift of salvation and keep us from God by deceiving men into breaking God's commandments. Don't let Satan win! Don't let him rob you of the salvation that God so graciously offers each one of us. Don't allow yourselves to be subject to government and religious leaders who deny the truth of God's word! Listen to the Lord. Webster's dictionary defines the word 'listen' as 'obedience.' Listen to the Lord and obey His word.

"Please read the handouts you received when you came in, and make copies for others if you can. Please share them!

"This is the last call, the very last opportunity to come to the Lord. There is no secret rapture, there is no second chance, only *right now*, to surrender your lives to Christ and serve Him. Today, if you hear His voice, harden not your hearts. *Today* is the day of salvation. If you truly love Him, take a firm stand on the side of His truth and He will give you the power to remain strong. He will protect and sustain you through all of the trials ahead, and reward your faithfulness with an eternity with Him in the place he has prepared for us.

"May the Lord keep you and uplift you through all that lies ahead on this brief journey to our eternal heavenly home. Amen."

"Amen," the crowd responded reverently.

After another hour of fellowship, prayer and praise, the crowd began to disperse and Phil and the others prepared to head back to the campsite. As they packed up the few remaining supplies, Phil and Jenny fought to hold back tears as they walked through the restaurant, gazing nostalgically at each room, more than likely for the very last time.

On their way back to the trailer, the two vehicles encountered a road block on the outskirts of town. Two officers were checking everyone's ID. No one was allowed to proceed without a state issued ID bracelet. Phil looked closely at the officer standing near a squad car on the other side of the roadblock, relieved to recognize his old friend, the newly promoted Captain Jackson.

"Jackson!" Phil shouted.

"Hey Phil," Captain Jackson replied, walking to the truck and leaning into the window. "What are you doing out here?"

"We're headed to our place out here and need to get through. What's with the road blocks?" Phil asked.

"We've been instructed to monitor all entrances into town," Jackson replied, glancing down at Phil's wrist. "By the looks of that bare wrist of yours, you haven't been documented yet."

"Documented? Forgive me for being out of the loop here, but we've all been camped out at my place for weeks. We haven't been anywhere but there and the restaurant a couple of times."

"Yeah, I'm afraid it's required. You'll have to report to one of the food stations or crisis centers to get a wristband."

"Come on Jackson," Phil pleaded. "We've got to get

home. Our families are out there, and if we have to go back into town and get documented we'll never make it back before dark. We can't be driving out at night Jackson, you know that."

"Well, you're right about that. Even I wouldn't want to be out here after curfew. You're a good man and a good friend, so just this once, I'm gonna let you through. But you'd better get into town and get those wristbands, or next time you're not going to be so lucky. These other guys aren't as sweet as I am, or as good looking." Jackson grinned, waving them forward.

"Thanks Jackson, you're a pal," Phil said as they drove past the roadblock, breathing a sigh of relief.

The evening meal was ready waiting for them when they arrived home, physically and emotionally exhausted.

"This is the last of the freezer food. I shut off the freezer to save the last little bit of gas in the generator's tank," Rick said. "How did it go today?"

"The restaurant was packed. I'd say about two-hundred people came today, wouldn't you Jenny?"

"I would guess nearly four-hundred total came and went throughout the day," Jenny said. "But around two-hundred in the building at any one time."

"They've blocked the roads," Steve said. "No one can enter or leave the city without an ID wristband. We only got through this time because Captain Jackson was at the roadblock and let us by, but we won't have that luxury again."

"Roadblocks are the least of our problems now," Rick

replied. "Martial law has been instituted throughout most countries. The UN, National guard and all four branches of the military have deployed teams of troops to eliminate the 'terrorists.' We'll be commanded to comply with the law or be jailed to await execution."

"Well we knew these days were coming, but I had no idea just how quickly it would all come to a head," Beth said.

"Time is short, that much is certain," Phil said. "We'd better call it a night so we can get an early start in the morning. We need to go hunt down some food or we'll starve before next weekend."

"I'll go with you," Eddie offered.

"Great, I'll see you in the morning," Phil replied, heading into the trailer, where he knelt by the bed in prayer. He prayed earnestly for all of those who had come to worship with them that day, as well as for each member of their little group in the woods. He plead for the Holy Spirit to be cured out on each one of them without measure, to cleanse them of their sins and prepare them for what was to come.

He slept soundly, unaware of the fierce, unseen battle raging around him or its rapid escalation to the final, fiery climax that would reveal once and for all where every member of the human race stood in this age-old controversy between Christ and Satan.

The End, The Beginning

Jenny and Phil lay in bed, wondering what the coming weeks would bring with the ongoing turmoil and shortage of food.

"I can't believe it has come to this," Phil said. "Just a couple months ago we were living comfortably, had a thriving restaurant that we worked so hard to establish, and for what? Everything is gone, the entire world has been turned upside down, and now we don't even have enough food to get through the week."

"Yes, and you can't afford to lose any more weight," Jenny said, hugging her slender man.

"I know; I'm down to 210 pounds. I found the scale at the restaurant and weighed in. Can you believe it?"

"That was the goal you wanted to reach!" Jenny squealed with excitement. "And to think that all you did was switch to a plant-based diet and begin walking every day."

"Yeah, it's really something, isn't it? But now this whole world is turned on its ear." Phil shook his head in discouragement.

"It's not the end, Phil," Jenny replied. "This is just the beginning! We have a whole eternity with our Savior waiting for us. Soon we will look back at these last days as our final steps to the kingdom."

"That's true Jenny, and I can't wait, but these last steps are some pretty difficult ones. We're going hunting in the morning, but I really don't want to. I really have no desire for any animal meat, and I dread the thought of having to shoot an animal."

"That's no surprise, after being without meat for all these years," Jenny replied. "You know, this is the berry season. I think I'll take the girls out to the lake tomorrow to search for berries."

"That's a great idea. I'll tell you what, Eddie and I will meet you at the dock on the south side of the lake after we're done hunting."

"I'll bring some food for a picnic." Jenny said, "But we'd better get a good night sleep."

"Good night my love," Phil said.

Phil lay in bed, thinking of the weight-loss journey that had taken him all those years of commitment.

…<<…

"Step on up Phil," Dr. Foster said, clapping Phil on the back with an encouraging smile. "Let's see what you've done."

Phil stepped on the scale and watched as the digital numbers blinked and changed beneath him. Finally, the scale beeped as it registered a final number. Phil looked down to see that he had lost 150 pounds. Mike, Jenny and Dr. Foster cheered as Phil stared at the number in amazement.

"You did it Phil!" Dr. Foster said. "Your weight is now 240 pounds!"

"I could still lose another 30 pounds or so," Phil said. "But the last 50 have taken me over two years to lose."

"Yes, the first pounds generally come off rather easy, but the last ones are always the toughest," Dr. Foster said.

"I'm so proud of you!" Jenny threw her arms around Phil and kissed his cheek.

"Thank you so much, Doc. You saved my life!" Phil said.

"And you too Mike. I couldn't have done this without all that great food and our daily walks."

Mike smiled. "It was my pleasure, Phil. And I think we need to go for that last 30 pounds and really show this community what God can do in their lives when they trust God and obey his principles for health."

"Amen!" Phil agreed.

"And not just you Phil," Dr. Foster said. "This is also about the people you've inspired to make changes. Did you know that over three-thousand local people have signed those commitment cards?"

"Really?" Phil's eyes widened in surprise. "I had no idea."

"And the thousand people who went through the entire program had lost an average of 32 pounds," Jenny added.

"And that's just the weight," Dr. Foster continued. "Just think of all the fantastic things it has done for everyone internally. People have reversed or drastically reduced diabetes, hypertension, heart disease and many other lifestyle related diseases."

"We can't thank you enough Dr. Foster," Jenny said. "If it wasn't for you taking care of Phil, who knows what might have happened."

"You know, I wasn't even supposed to be at the hospital that week," Dr. Foster recalled. "I was scheduled to be at a convention in Indiana, but my flight was canceled because of the blizzard. Remember that crazy storm?"

"I sure do, because we got the tail end of it." Phil said, "I was out there every morning shoveling all that snow."

"What's more, I wasn't even supposed to be in the ER." Dr. Foster said.

"Really?" Jenny asked.

"No, I don't do ER work, never have. But there was one problem after another at the hospital and with no one to cover shifts, they started calling local doctors. Since my office is at the medical center connected to the hospital, they called me out of sheer desperation. Since my trip was canceled, I offered to cover at the hospital for the week."

Phil smiled. "God really does work in amazing ways."

"He sure does," Dr. Foster replied. "In fact, as much as I was being used by God to give you a health message, He was using you to bring me the truth about the Sabbath. If not for you, my family would still be following the traditions of man rather than the commandments of God."

"Amen to that," Mike said. "It is simply amazing to see how God orchestrates our lives. With us as individuals and with global events as we see prophesy being fulfilled time and time again."

"And here we are looking at the last day prophecy coming to full completion right now." Phil added.

"Simply amazing." Jenny said. "We just can't comprehend the power of God's love."

"And grace," Mike added.

"And mercy," Dr. Foster said. "Oh, the mercy He pours out on us, undeserving though we are."

"Well, we've got a big day tomorrow with the last health class of this fifth season," Phil said. "I think we'd better call it a night and get some sleep."

...>>...

Phil awoke early the next morning, feeling well rested in spite of last night's reminiscing. He slipped quietly out of bed and crept to the living room. Steve was just waking up, so he and Phil sat down to check the news together while the others enjoyed an extra bit of sleep. They were enjoying a reprieve from earthquakes and tornados, but they knew this was just the calm before the storm. They also knew from the news that the rest of the planet was in the midst of the worst natural disasters the world had ever seen. The two men sat shaking their heads as they watched the reports come in from around the globe.

"Look at the sickness everywhere, and now plagues," Phil said.

"No toilets, no fresh water, dead bodies not even being buried," Steve added.

"And they thought Ebola was bad," Phil said. "Just look at these other plagues that are so widespread."

Steve nodded. "There's just not enough manpower to deal with all the chaos and disaster. It's happening exponentially, just like birthing pains. The world doesn't even recover from one tragedy before another one erupts."

As Phil reached for the remote to switch off the television, a man with a bayonet rifle charged around the corner of the barn. Startling him could have produced a horrible outcome if he'd had an itchy trigger finger, but this man was more cautious and paranoid than anything. Phil stood and looked at the man, realizing from his clothing that he was one of the Peacekeepers, the special militarized unit assigned to deal with the "rebels."

"Can I help you?" Phil said.

"Who are you?" The man asked, his eyes narrowing suspiciously. He looked as if he couldn't be older than twenty-five years old.

"I'm the owner of this property."

"You need to come with me!" The Peacekeeper said sharply.

Phil stepped slowly and carefully toward the young man and said calmly, "I don't need to go anywhere."

The Peacekeeper glanced at Phil's wrist. Not seeing a bracelet, he assumed he was an undocumented terrorist.

"I have to arrest you," he said.

"For what?" Phil asked. "We haven't done anything

wrong."

As Phil took another step closer to the Peacekeeper to explain, the young man panicked and lunged the bayonet into Phil's chest.

"Phil!" Jenny, who had been watching from the door of the trailer, screamed and ran toward her husband.

The Peacekeeper pulled the bayonet out and turned to plunge it into Steve, who was moving toward him, but the weapon was mangled and twisted as though it was made of straw. Phil clutched his chest and realized that there was no wound. The bayonet had done him no harm. The young man's eyes widened in confusion and terror. He turned and fled back toward the troops, blowing furiously on an alert whistle.

Phil scrambled to his feet and ran with Steve and Jenny to open the barn doors and wake the others.

"We've got trouble!" Steve shouted as Phil shut and latched the barn doors.

They sat in the silent darkness, waiting for the Peacekeeper to return with his troops.

They didn't have to wait long. The barn doors burst open and Peacekeepers rushed in, flashlights sweeping across the room. Phil and the others sat frozen, waiting to be arrested and dragged off the property. The men's lights swept over their faces over and over again, but no one made a move toward the group. "There's nobody in here," the troop leader growled. "Let's move on." The men exited the barn and drove off toward the woods, leaving the group in a shocked and confused huddle.

They stayed in the barn, praying quietly for hours until the hungry children could wait no more. Phil cracked the barn door open slowly, looking around for any remaining Peacekeepers before leading the group out of the barn and over to the trailer for something to eat.

Most of the group spent the rest of the day in front of the television watching the never-ending reports of devastation being experienced around the world. Peaceful, innocent people were being portrayed as rebels and terrorists for disobeying government directives. Obedience to the Fourth Commandment automatically put a bounty on one's head. Dragged off like criminals, some were held captive while others were assassinated on the spot, to the cheers of onlookers. All because of the desperation of a dying world completely and irreversibly deceived by Satan.

The men took turns keeping an eye on the road, watching for another sweep of Peacekeeper troops in the area. Over the next few days, the news brought more unrest with increasing global problems. With too many catastrophes to keep up with, most of the reports were directed toward trying to establish unity and peace. Ironically, the Peacekeepers were ramping up their efforts to kill anyone who was against their directives. The urgency of eliminating dissenters took center stage. Everyone was encouraged to turn in anyone suspected of unauthorized activity. Even friends and family members were now turning against one another. Like sheep blindly headed to the slaughter, the world's inhabitants were working directly against the God they claimed to serve.

The little band of believers at Phil and Jenny's property gathered together in prayer morning, noon and night. What else was there to do but hang their helpless souls on Christ and trust in His hand of protection.

Their food provisions had dwindled down to almost

nothing, and going to town for more was not an option. They knew from recent news reports that hunger had become a global problem. Shipping had come to a standstill, and most stores were closed, their shelves bare and aisles empty. The hungry were searching out every possible morsel of food, and any stored provisions were confiscated by the authorities. The group had finished off all but the very last of the oatmeal and rice, and knew that they would soon be wholly dependent on the Lord for sustenance.

One week after their run in with the Peacekeepers, the group huddled quietly around a small battery operated radio in the barn and heard reports that people disappearing all over the world. Some people were claiming that the rapture had occurred, but were quickly shouted down by those who believed that if the rapture had come, they surely would have been taken. Besides, there were no reports of people vanishing into thin air and leaving behind their clothing behind. Something else was happening, but no one could say just what or why.

"Remember when the guards came in here and didn't see us?" Steve asked. "Well, according to them, *we* have disappeared."

"That's right. God has 'hidden' us from them to keep us safe," Phil said.

"Look how furious they are, trying to find these people that they are never going to find," Beth sighed, shaking her head.

The power was gone, and there was no more fuel to cook, and the batteries in the radio finally died out. With no more food, there was nothing left to do but pray and try to sleep. Once more, the group gathered to pray before going to bed.

"Lord we need you," Steve prayed. "We have come to the end of our resources. The food is gone and our stomachs growl with hunger. We know that you are the provider of all things and we trust in You with every fiber of our beings. You provided manna for forty years, and we know that you will provide for us in the morning hour. Give us this day, our daily bread. Give us the true Bread, for You are the Bread of Life. We ask You to dwell in our hearts and draw us ever closer to You. We love You Lord. In Jesus' name, Amen."

"Amen," the others echoed. Hungry but trusting in the promises of a faithful God, they drifted off to sleep.

Just before sunrise the next morning, Phil was suddenly awakened by a bright shaft of light streaming in though a crack in the barn door. Fearing the return of the Peacekeepers, he sat up quickly and began to pray, when suddenly he heard a voice saying "Get up, and go into the hills, to the place that I will show you. The time of your deliverance is at hand." As quickly as it had come, the light was gone, leaving Phil wondering for a moment if he had been dreaming. Crying out to God for wisdom, he was immediately filled with a sense of urgency, and quickly set about waking the others, telling them what he had seen and heard.

"What should we gather to take with us?" Steve asked.

"Nothing," Phil replied. There is nothing here that we need, and we have to move quickly, unencumbered. Just throw on your warmest clothes and let's get going."

The group hurried out into the cold, dark morning. The children sleepily rubbed their eyes, but asked no questions. Everyone sensed the spirit of God guiding them and felt a deep, abiding peace, despite the uncertainty of the situation.

"Which way should we go?" Jenny asked, shivering in the early morning air.

"I'm not sure yet," Phil replied. "But I know the Lord will show us where He wants us to go. Let's ask Him."

The group knelt in a small stand of trees, recommitting themselves to God and asking Him to lead and care for them.

As they opened their eyes, they saw a softly lit path leading into the trees to their right.

Looking at one another with smiles of astonished joy, they headed into the woods and up the path laid out for them, leading into the rugged hills above. As the path turned, hiding them in the trees, they heard the rumble of trucks below. Looking back, they peered through the faint pre-dawn light, making out the dim outline of three large military vehicles loaded with Peacekeepers coming up the road toward the barn. The group watched in shock as several shadowy figures hopped off of the trucks and kicked in the barn door, firing a hail of bullets into the now empty structure.

After firing for several seconds, another troop came behind them with several large barrels of gasoline, dousing the barn, then lighting it as they ran toward the trailer, where they repeated the arson.

With sinking hearts, Phil and the others watched the buildings burst into flames. Within seconds, they were fully engulfed, thick pillars of smoke rising ominously into the air. Tears filled their eyes as they looked at one another in disbelief.

"We were just moments from being burned alive," Eddie gasped.

Edith smiled, her gaze lifting skyward as she recited from Psalm 91.

"'He who dwells in the secret place of the Most High Shall abide under the shadow of the Almighty. I will say of the Lord, "He is my refuge and my fortress; My God, in Him I will trust." Surely He shall deliver you from the snare of the fowler and from the perilous pestilence.'"

Several of the others joined in.

"'He shall cover you with His feathers, and under His wings you shall take refuge; His truth shall be your shield and buckler. You shall not be afraid of the terror by night, Nor of the arrow that flies by day, nor of the pestilence that walks in darkness, nor of the destruction that lays waste at noonday.

"'A thousand may fall at your side, and ten thousand at your right hand; but it shall not come near you...'"

They paused as they heard the trucks driving off of the property. The Peacekeepers believed their mission was successful, and Phil and the others in the group were now presumed dead.

The hill was growing steeper and the path narrower, twisting and turning around the mountain ridge. They held on to one another, each person taking hold of the coat of the person in front of them. Eventually, it grew so narrow that they had to hug the rock face to stay upright. One misstep would have sent them tumbling into the ravine. Rocks tumbled down between their feet as they scrambled to keep their footing.

"'For He shall give His angels charge over you, to keep

you in all your ways. In their hands they shall bear you up, lest you dash your foot against a stone,'" Edith continued reciting as they climbed.

"'Because he has set his love upon Me, therefore I will deliver him; I will set him on high, because he has known My name. He shall call upon Me, and I will answer him; I will be with him in trouble; I will deliver him and honor him. With long life I will satisfy him, and show him My salvation.'"

They climbed for hours, singing hymns and reciting scripture to pass the hours as they followed the glowing path.

As they crested the hill, they came to a small, relatively flat clearing beneath an outcropping of rock jutting out from the hillside. Beneath the outcropping the side of the mountain hollowed into a little cave, providing shelter. The path ended, and the light circled the clearing. They had arrived at their place of refuge. Weary and out of breath, they were grateful for the opportunity to rest at last.

Steve climbed to the top of the outcropping. Glancing at his watch, he saw that it was nearly 4pm. They had been climbing for eleven hours! Strangely, although they had hiked all day, it had remained dark in the hills, their way lit only by the faint light of the glowing path before them. God had shrouded them in semi-darkness, preventing them from being seen from below. Now that they had reached the top, he could clearly see daylight above him, but below him in the clearing, the group was cast in a shadow. Steve leaned forward and peered down the mountainside, gasping at the sight before him. Scattered around the surrounding hills were dozens of softly glowing paths. There were others taking refuge in these hills, all of them waiting for deliverance.

Climbing back down to join the group, Steve was met by Mickey, begging for something to eat. Steve was explaining to his son that they simply didn't have any food when he saw Lisa approaching, her arms loaded down with as many apples as she could hold.

"Look, Steve! There are apple trees just past the clearing, and a blackberry bush, too! It doesn't make sense that they would be growing way up here, but here they are!"

Beth and Sally were just behind her, laden down with fruit. "We need something to put the berries in," Beth said. "And volunteers to help us pick more, too!"

Eric and Eddie stood quickly and headed in the direction of the bushes. "We'll help pick," Eric offered.

"I'll help too," Rick said. "The more of us picking, the sooner we can fill these kids' growling tummies."

"You can put the berries in this and tie the corners together," Phil said, handing them a large plaid flannel shirt. "I wore several extra layers, but I'm still warm from the climb."

Terri and Kimmie set to work clearing rocks, leaves and other debris from the cave floor.

"I'm going back for more apples," Lisa said.

"Mama, I'm so thirsty, is there any water to drink?" Mickey asked.

"I'm sorry sweetie, we don't have any," Lisa replied. "It's funny, I wasn't even thirsty on the trail, but now I'm parched. I guess we'll just have to —"

Just then, a trickle of clear, fresh water began streaming from the rock wall on the outside of the cave.

"Mama, water!" Mickey exclaimed, running toward the miraculous stream, with Beth's girls Abby and Megan close behind him. The adults stood back and let the children drink first. They had all been so patient and uncomplaining during the long climb up the mountain.

"This is the best water I've ever tasted," Megan said, swiping an arm across her ripping mouth.

"It's so cold and sweet!" Abby squealed.

After everyone had a chance to drink until they were satisfied, the water slowed to barely a trickle, then stopped. They all ate their fill of the apples and blackberries, then rested against the walls inside the little cave.

"Can you believe that?" Phil asked, shaking his head in astonishment. "Water from the side of a mountain, and the most delicious fruit I've ever tasted, right in the middle of the evergreens!"

"And the perfect place to rest and stay out of view," Jenny added. The Lord really has provided us with everything we need."

"We picked the apple tree and blackberry bush clean, and there was just enough for all of us, but I'm afraid there's nothing left for us to eat tomorrow," Lisa said.

Andy, the elderly gentleman Phil had brought back from the restaurant, leaned his head back against the rock wall and smiled as he quoted Isaiah 33:16. *"'He will dwell on high; His place of defense will be the fortress of rocks; Bread will be given him, His water will be sure.'"*

"He certainly has kept His word, hasn't he dear?" Florence

said, taking Andy's hand.

"Yes my love, and He will continue to do so. I have no doubt that tomorrow, and every day until He comes, our needs will be provided just as faithfully as today. Don't you worry, Lisa, there will be food again tomorrow!"

The group sat for several hours in silent prayer, each one searching their hearts for any unconfessed, unrepented sin, though none of them could think of anything for which they had not already sought forgiveness. They were unaware that some time ago, the decree had already been made in Heaven:

"He who is unjust, let him be unjust still; he who is filthy, let him be filthy still; he who is righteous, let him be righteous[e] still; he who is holy, let him be holy still.

"And behold, I am coming quickly, and My reward is with Me, to give to every one according to his work." Revelation 12:11,12

That night, they all slept comfortably, despite having to lie on the cold, hard ground. The next morning, they arose and set about picking more fruit and again, there was just enough to feed them all, with nothing left over. The water also reappeared for as long as it took to quench their thirsts before receding once again into the mountainside.

A week went by, during which time the little group in the mountains experienced extraordinary fellowship and peace. Occasionally, the sound of gunfire or explosions would reach them, and plumes of smoke could be seen drifting across the sky below.

One morning, Lisa rose early to begin gathering fruit for breakfast. As she returned with the first load of blackberries, she heard a strange sound coming from somewhere down the mountain. As she listened, she soon detected the sound of boots crunching on the rocks. Lots of boots. Coming fast! Turning quickly, she dropped the flannel shirt full of berries and ran toward the cave, fruit scattering across the ground.

Lisa entered the cave and went straight to her sleeping husband. Grabbing Steve's arm and shaking him awake, she called out in a loud whisper, "Steve! Steve, wake up! The Peacekeepers are coming up the mountain. They've found us; they know where we are!"

Steve sat up, immediately alert. "I don't think they know it's us up here," he said. "They think we're dead, remember? They must be doing a sweep of the mountains looking for hidden 'rebels.' Either way, there's nothing we can do but pray."

Barely had the words left Steve's mouth when two Peacekeepers ducked into the cave's entrance, the bright beams of their flashlights sweeping across the sleeping group, then landing on Steve and Lisa."

"Get up, you lousy rebels! Your time is up. You're finally going to get what you deserve," one of them sneered as the other grabbed Steve by the arm and dragged him toward the entrance.

The rest of the group awoke, startled by the scene. Mickey jumped up and ran toward his father.

"Daddy! No, don't hurt my Daddy!" He pleaded, clinging to Steve's leg. The Peacekeeper yanked him off and set him back on the ground.

"Don't worry son, you're not in trouble," the man said. "All children under the age of twelve will be taken to reeducation centers to be deprogrammed and integrated into society. You'll be taught to renounce the dangerous, false ideas your parents have forced on you." He gestured to the other trooper, who quickly stepped in to hold Mickey back as Steve was hauled outside where the rest of the troop waited just outside the cave's entrance with guns raised, ready to fire.

"We have express orders to shoot any and all adult rebels, the man explained to the group. The children will come with us as soon as you're all taken care of. Now, everyone come on out slowly, with your hands in the air, and don't do anything stupid. You'll only make things worse."

They made their way out of the cave to the clearing, where Steve knelt on the ground, the Peacekeeper standing over him with a gun to his temple.

"Steve!" Lisa fell to the ground, pulling Mickey into her arms and turning him away from the awful scene.

The peacekeeper cocked his gun and leaned in close to Steve's face. "This is what happens to those who would disturb the peace and safety of others in selfish pursuit of their own ideas," he said.

Lisa looked down at Mickey to see him staring over her shoulder at something in the sky. She turned to follow his gaze and saw a small black cloud in the distance, about as big as a man's fist. The cloud was moving, growing steadily as it came closer. The others turned and watched also as the strange little cloud approached.

The ground beneath them began to tremble, the sky grew dark and the cloud drew closer, now appearing lighter in color. As they watched, the cloud came to life with thousands upon thousands of bright, glorious beings, and the sound of trumpets filled the air. The Peacekeepers were frozen in terror at the sight, while the group of believers knelt to the ground, tears of joy streaming down their faces, a rainbow encircling them as they gazed at the glorious sight.

The cloud was now brilliant with the light of the angels, causing the Peacekeepers to drop their guns and raise their arms to their faces, shielding their eyes. The troopers turned to flee, several of them scrambling down the hill, amid the tumbling rocks. As the ground trembled even more violently, the overhang of rock above the cave cracked and snapped off, falling onto the heads of the men beneath it, though no one else noticed.

The voices of the angels filled the air, and a loud voice called "Awake! Awake ye that sleep in the dust!"

At that shout, thousands of graves were opened and the faithful from all generations rose from their slumber, escorted by heavenly angels into the air.

The group felt themselves rising, and looked to see angels at their sides, guiding them toward the Savior. They gazed at one another is amazement at the transformation that had taken place. Edith, Andy and Florence were young and strong, but still fully recognizable. They all felt perfect health and vitality surge through their now perfect bodies. An angel approached Lisa and gently placed a tiny, perfect baby in her arms. Lisa held the infant to her chest, weeping with unspeakable joy and gratitude. Steve placed an arm around her and Mickey as they were all drawn up together, reunited at last.

Phil and Jenny clung to one another as they ascended toward the cloud, looking into the face of Jesus, whose eyes shone back at them with an expression of deepest love.

As Phil and Jenny continued to gaze at the Savior, it

seemed as though they were looking once again at Mike. Could it be? Had it actually been Jesus all those years, teaching and guiding them in the truth? Those eyes, that expression - *was that their Mike?* After all, there was Mike, coming in the clouds of glory. But as they looked around at the multitudes of others who knew Him too, they realized that it wasn't actually Mike up there, but Christ alone. And then they understood that they had never really seen Mike at all - the face they had seen all those years, the eyes full of such compassion, sympathy and genuine love was merely the reflection of Christ, the Master Chef, shining through Mike all along.

Made in the USA
Middletown, DE
17 February 2023

25015194R00142